# THE WHISKEY WAR

## NINJANS 5

Dave Kwan

# DISCLAIMER



Front Cover Artwork by aheflin - Adobe Stock

File#: 219712287   JPEG   2669 x 4000px



ISBN:
ISBN-13: 978-1-990257-04-9

# DEDICATION

This book is dedicated to
**SUSAN  SIZE**
of London, Ontario.
A woman who is a remarkable
wife, mother, businesswoman;
and a lady of faith.
Sue is a cherished friend to our family!

# CHAPTER ONE

## *The Terrible Traders*

### SCENE

A rickety old wagon laden with wood barrels, creaks along the rugged trail heading for higher elevation. The noonday sun is scorching hot, baking the wilderness like an oven. Out in the barren landscape, the wind blows across the hot sand, scruffy brush, and short gnarled trees. This is the natural habitat of the fox, jack rabbit, hawk, and coyote. The wagon belongs more in town that out in the wild tundra. The large spoked wheels roll over small rocks strewn across the path. The wagon follows the shallow ruts, grooves worn into the rock by other wagons from a previous time. As the wagon goes up the incline, BADGER, the driver, snaps the whip. CRACK, and yells, "Move it you mangy critters!" The four mules tug and strain to move the heavy load up the rocky slope. Badger snaps the whip. CRACK. CRACK. The mules struggle to get footing on the smooth rock surface. Finally, the wagon and team of mules reach the top of the Butte. The trail ahead is flat and easier to manage for the men transporting their cargo to its destination. The driver pulls on the harness for the mules to stop, and he pushes the wood lever to set the brake. The two men climb down from the wagon seat to stand on the ground and stretch. Badger is a big old grizzled muleskinner, with a shaggy beard and two missing front teeth. The story is Badger lost the teeth in a Bar fight at a Mining Camp. His trail partner, GRIT, is a tall lean man, who once worked as a Railroad Enforcer, scaring and beating Railway workers, turning them into cowering submissive labourers. As the mules rest, the men look in the direction they're headed. Badger spits out chewing tobacco and remarks, "I don't see them! Not a one." Grit puts his hand to his eyebrows and squints his eyes, "Partner, you're right! Nothing. Nobody. (Pause) Do you think we're too early?" The big man lumbers to the front of the mule team and looks again, "I don't see a thing. No horses. No riders!" He turns about to rejoin his partner. Grit glances at Badger and comments, "What are we going to do?" Badger lowers and sits down in the shaded portion of the wagon, and replies, "They'll show up. Guaranteed! (Wipes sweat from brow) After all, (Pats Barrel) we got what they want!" Grit hunkers down beside Badger, and grins as he remarks, "This is gonna make us rich! Badger points to the barrels and responds, "Yes Siree - All we have to do is keep 'em supplied!" Both men chuckle with a sinister grin. Grit groans, "This sun has me parched! I need a drink." The tall man stands to his feet and yanks on the canvass tarp covering a wood crate filled with bottles. Grit grabs a bootle and pulls off the cork with his teeth - raises his arm and takes a deep guzzle - AHHHH! Grit wipes the booze from his lips and remarks, "Whiskey! There's nothing like it!" He hands the bottle to Badger, who tilts his head back to take a long drink that drains half the bottle. Badger quips, "Whiskey is like liquid gold - We're the only ones willing to sell it. Sell every drop. Indian money is as good as any!" They both gloat and laugh. Badger picks up the cork in the dirt, wipes it off, and seals up the bottle.

The Butte's elevation offers a commanding vista of the land that lays below. Badger looks out at some vultures circling in the sky above a animal carcass laying on the ground. The large scavenger birds have wide wing spans that enable them to soar and glide effortlessly, circling lower and lower, until the vultures eventually land beside the carcass, only to poke and prod the remains for any signs of life. With no response, the vultures crowd in to devour the remains, leaving just bare bones as a sign of their work. The noonday sun is high overhead, the temperature terrible for man and beast. Badger and Grit know from previous experience, not to exert effort or do anything strenuous at this time of day. The people in Mexico, Texas, and Arizona, know the wisdom of staying in the shade, keeping out from the burning sun. Badger and Grit will simply sit in the shaded portion of the wagon, and wait. The two Whiskey Traders know of those desperate for what they have - barrels and barrels of cheap Whiskey - enough booze to intoxicate and numb the soul - enough liquor for an entire Indian Camp.

* * *

Badger lifts his gaze and notices a cloud of dust in the distance, dust from approaching horses. The gruff man gets his partner's attention, "Grit. Get ready! Riders are coming." Both men stand to their feet and walk to the front of the mule team to watch the riders heading toward them. Grit turns to Badger and remarks, "Looks like we're in business, partner!" Badger stares at the riders getting closer, he spits a stream of chewing tobacco onto the dusty ground, then replies, "I see a big group of riders. Get the bottles ready!" Grit walks to the back of the wagon, grabs an empty burlap sack and fills it with 10 Whiskey bottles, then returns to stand beside Badger. By now, it's clearly visible that the group of riders are forty Indian braves. These are young bucks ready for action and adventure, and seek the thrills that whiskey has the power to give.

The group of Indian braves stop their horses 100 yards from the wagon. The young braves sit on their mounts and stare at Badger and Grit with expressionless faces. These young bucks carry rifles, spears, tomahawks, as well as bows and arrows. Their leader is a cantankerous hot-head brave called "STORM CLOUD". A young muscle-bound warrior known for his bad temper and volatile nature. Storm Cloud earned his name years ago from the many fights he had with other braves. Once, he killed a brave during a terrible fight. Storm Cloud lifted his opponent high above his head, only to be brought down hard across his knee - snapping his opponent's back, killing him instantly. It was said, Storm Cloud looked at the Indian braves gathered to watch, and remarked, "Anyone one else want to challenge my leadership?" All the braves feared his wrath, everyone stayed silent. That incident was a couple years ago. Now, Storm Cloud is a more experienced leader with a growing number of young warriors. He's a force to be reckoned with, and someone who is dangerous and deadly!

Badger and Grit step out from alongside the mules and walk to within 100 paces of the cluster of Indian braves. Storm Cloud raises his hand and yells out in English, "Enough! Stop!" Badger and his partner immediately halt their stride and stand still. Storm Cloud eyes the two white men and demands, "Want Whiskey!" Badger grins and replies, "We have your sack of Whiskey." The young Indian leader brings his mount out a few paces to get closer. Storm Cloud turns to gaze at his warriors, then looks at the Traders, "More Whiskey. 2 sacks!" Grit whispers to Badger, "We don't have enough bottles for 2 sacks! What are we gonna do?" Badger turns to Grit and replies, "We give 'em a barrel! That's the only way to keep 'em happy." With the eyes of the Indian braves fixed on the Traders, Badger looks at Storm Cloud, and points to the wagon, "You can have more Whiskey - take a Barrel!" The countenance of the young leader changes from stone-face to a wide smile, "Much Whiskey better!" Storm Cloud orders a couple nearby braves to ride to the wagon and retrieve a wood barrel. The two braves bolt their horses forward, reach the wagon and grab a barrel off the back. Riding side-by-side, the two braves bring the Whiskey barrel up to Storm Cloud. The young man's eyes light up at seeing the Whiskey barrel close up. He looks at Badger and Grit, and remarks with a grin, "Storm Cloud like Barrel!" The young warrior tosses a leather pouch of gold coins to Badger, then waves his arm in the air; the group of warriors turn their horses around and head off with loud YELLS and WAR CRIES. Storm Cloud rides beside the two braves transporting the Whiskey Barrel. As the young bucks get further away in the distance, Badger turns to Grit with pouch of coins in hand, and grins, "That's what I call 'Wetting' the Appetite! (Pause) Those braves will be back for more and more." Grit grins with glee, "More Whiskey means more money. I say we're gonna be rich, Amigo!" The two Traders mosey back to the wagon, climb up and get seated. Badger grabs the whip and gives it a SNAP! The mules jolt alert and begin to pull the wagon out across the dusty ground of the rugged wilderness.

The two Traders are not alone in this venture. Badger and Grit belong to a loose ragtag group of sketchy Traders based in a wilderness patch known as **Dry Gulch**. Simply put, Dry Gulch, is an assortment of ramshackle wood huts, buildings, and tents, grouped together to form what some might call a wilderness collective, or a Traders' haven. There, the men can sleep, eat, store supplies, have camaraderie, and protect each others' backs. These are Traders who travel to and fro across the Great Plains to ply their wares to towns, ranches, farms, railroad camps, and stagecoach stops. Many of these are rough characters like Badger and Grit. There's a mutual understanding between the Traders, and each Trader respects the other's operation. Everyone is aware that Badger and Grit are selling Whiskey to Storm Cloud. He's their customer - theirs alone. The Trader Code at Dry Gulch is that no one meddles with another Trader's business, if anyone does - it's at the risk of being knifed in your sleep, or shot dead and your carcass left in the wilderness for the Vultures and Coyotes. Even though, Badger and Grit are the ones trading Whiskey with Storm Cloud, if there's any trouble - all Traders and all their guns have their backs.

5

The Traders of Dry Gulch come from all walks of what some would call 'another life'. These men are - ex-soldiers, rough railroad workers, old Cowboys, former prisoners, grizzled miners, and one-time merchants. Regardless of the background, all the Traders at Dry Gulch are money-hungry and greedy for gold - even if it means breaking Territory Law to sell Whiskey to Indians.

# CHAPTER TWO

## *Rogue Warriors*

Storm Cloud and his band of young warriors return to their Camp - a cluster of Tepees and canvass shelters set up near the base of a cliff. The young braves are excited to taste Whiskey once again. Storm Cloud orders the Barrel be placed in the middle of the Tepees, and tells a brave to turn the barrel upright and crack open the top. The broken wood top is pried away exposing a full barrel of liquor, the young warriors gather with heightened excitement, ready and eager to drink their fill. There's jostling and shoving as the braves crowd around the open Barrel, dipping in their tin cups and clay bowls to scoop up the amber liquor. The young men repeatedly down the liquor, and soon begin to feel the effects of alcohol. The young braves let out loud SHOUTS, YELLS, and WAR CRIES, as they begin to stomp the ground in Tribal Dance. Storm Cloud watches with a big grin because he knows that once his warriors are filled with booze, they will do his bidding without question. This time, Storm Cloud has set his sights on a big Ranch where there's plenty of cattle to take. A brave brings him a hollow gourd filled with Whiskey, and the Leader tilts his head back and downs the liquid. He wipes his lips, looks around with delight at his drunken warriors. The braves are drunk on liquor - while Storm Cloud is 'Drunk on Power'!

The brash young leader mounts his horse, spins the animal in a circle, and YELLS at the top of his lungs, "Warriors - Get your weapons! We raid the big Cattle Ranch!" The young braves with liquored bravado and frenzied excitement, grab weapons and horses, and quickly form the Raiding Party ready to do Storm Cloud's bidding. The braves are rambunctious and rowdy - the adrenaline courses through their veins, as liquor flows through their bodies. The young leader raises his arm high and motions - the group of armed drunken braves bolt their horses forward with YELLS, SCREAMS, and WAR CRIES!

# CHAPTER THREE

## *Raid on the Double J Ranch*

Thousands of cattle are spread across sections of rolling grassland on the Great Plains. Cowboys ride herd to guide the bovines from pasture to pasture. The cattle operation belongs to the big Double J Ranch, pioneered and developed by a tough seasoned cattleman named, Joshua Eli Jones. As a young cowboy, Joshua dreamed of someday owning his own spread. The young man worked hard and long to save wages, until he was able to buy a small parcel of land and a few cattle. From those humble beginnings, Joshua started to build his dream. Through persistence, diligence, shrewd bargaining, and an uncanny eye for good cattle, Joshua Eli Jones built a cattle empire. The enterprise and its cattle brand bears tribute to his pioneering spirit - the Double J stands for "Joshua Jones". The Ranch has over 100 cowboys that hale from Wild West places like - Texas, Arizona, Kansas, Oklahoma, Utah, and Mexico. A few cowboys are from Bandera, Texas; which is one of the staging grounds for big Cattle Drives along the Great Western Trail (also called the Old Texas Trail). Ranchers took that route when driving their large herds to the railhead in Dodge City, Kansas. Once there, the Ranchers were able to sell their cattle for meat, hides, and tallow (animal fat). Up north in Wyoming, the Double J Ranch is rich with its own cowboy heritage, the Double J Brand and reputation is known far and wide, even on Ranches down in Texas.

The Ranch grew to become a complex of buildings, barns, corals, and work sheds. A large two-story granite house with a wide veranda is the Boss's official residence. It sits in the centre, surrounded by bunkhouses and barns, that store feed, tackle, and supplies. Corals and holding pens lay on the outer perimeter. To see the entire ranch would take a couple days, there are so many different pastures spread out. In its entire history, the Double J Ranch's massive cattle operation never had any trouble from the Indian Tribes. A mutual respect and admiration was shared between Joshua and the different Indian Chiefs. The shared understanding was "Live and Let Live!" - Everyone, whether paleface or Indian, lived peaceably side-by-side, tending to their own way of life. It was this stable, peaceful co-existence, that Storm Cloud really wanted to steal away, not just the cattle. The headstrong young warrior reasoned - if trouble was created with the White Man, - he could rally hundreds of braves for a big War Party - a War Party willing to follow Storm Cloud as their new Chief!

The Cowboys have the steers settled quiet in the #48 North Pasture. Many of the cattle in the herd stand motionless, while some animals slowly move about here and there. The men have worked a long hard day, and gather around a campfire with a kettle of coffee on the brew. The Ranch hands look forward to getting some rest, share some conversation, and enjoy a nice cup of coffee. A few Cowboys sit on their horses to watch over the herd. All seems well.

Suddenly, burning arrows land in the ground near the cattle - the fire spooks the animals - the terrified cattle jostle about and start to stampede, the entire herd rushing the wire fence. The strong hooves of three hundred cattle flatten the wire fence in their path. The Cowboys on watch sound the Alarm! - "STAMPEDE! STAMPEDE! INDIANS!" The men around the campfire jump into action, quickly grab their horses, mount up and chase after the loose cattle. As the Cowboys gain ground closing in on the stampeding herd - two separate groups of Indian warriors intercept their pursuit, one from the right and one from the left. The mass of young warriors fire arrows and rifles at the Cowboys. Three Ranch hands get hit with arrows and gunshot, one dies. The Cowboys return fire, shooting their pistols and Winchester rifles. Greatly outnumbered, the Double J Cowboys turn and high-tail it, putting distance between the arrows and bullets from the Warriors. The young braves ride to catch the herd, their large numbers easily control the cattle, leading the animals down into a Gulley where the braves hold and keep the restless bovine. Storm Cloud rides to the crest of the slope and eyes the cattle herd - stolen trophies of his Raid. A warrior rides up beside the young leader and states, "We are ready!" Storm Cloud waves his arm and orders, "Move the Cattle to our

Canyon!" The brave rides off, and in a matter of minutes, the entire herd is moved by Indian riders. They guide the animals across the rugged tundra, deep into Indian territory, and through the rocky formations, where Storm Cloud has chosen a remote dead-end Canyon to secretly hide the cattle. The hundreds of head of cattle are enclosed by the Canyon walls, and the Indians place thorn bushes at the open end to barricade the animals in. Storm Cloud and the rest of his braves set up Camp near the Canyon entrance. Indian warriors are posted to guard the Camp and watch over the herd.

Back at the Double J Ranch, as the wounded Cowboys get tended to in the Bunkhouse, the lead wrangler, "Cody", and the Cowboys look at Joshua Jones as he stands on the main house big veranda. The Ranch owner asks in a puzzled tone, "You say Indians attacked you?" Cody replies, "They came out of nowhere - stole the herd, and shot at us with arrows and rifles (Pause) Jesse was killed!" Joshua is stunned, "Jesse's dead!" Cody comments, "Yes Sir!" The Rancher shakes his head with sadness, "Jesse was with me from the start! It's hard to believe he's gone." Cody takes a step forward, "Boss. Let me go to the other Ranchers - we'll get lots of guns, go after the Indians and get back our herd!" The other cowboys voice their support. Joshua looks at his men and remarks, "Don't get the other Ranchers involved! This is our concern - ours only." Cody pipes up, "But Boss - we lost hundreds of cattle!" Joshua steps down from the veranda to get close to the Ranch hands, and comments in a sober tone, "Better to loose hundreds of cattle that to loose hundreds of men. No! We'll keep the other Ranchers out of it. (Eyes men) That's all!" The older man ascends the steps of the veranda, turns about and looks firmly at Cody and the others. Cody glances at his fellow Ranch hands, then remarks, "You got it Boss! Your Cattle - your loss." Joshua smiles and replies, "No Cattle can replace a man's life! (Looks at men) I don't want to loose any of you men! (Grins) Where else could I get such good Ranch hands!" Joshua's comment makes Cody and the other men grin, and Cody remarks, "Good night Boss!" The Cowboys turn about and head to the Bunkhouse. Joshua watches the crew walk toward the big long structure, he gives a SIGH of relief that trouble was averted. Joshua turns around and enters inside the Main house.

A couple days later, Joshua and some ranch hands ride to a nearby Indian Village to meet with the Tribe's Chief and Elders. As Joshua and the Tribe's Chief and leaders enter into the large tepee to talk, the ranch hands patiently wait outside. After what seems a long time, Joshua exits the tepee with the Chief and Elders. The Rancher shakes hands with the Tribe's Chief, then mounts his horse and sits in the saddle. He looks at the Chief and Elders and waves bye, then turns to ride out of the Indian Camp. As Joshua and his men ride out, a Cowboy leans over to ask, "What did you talk about, Boss?" Joshua turns to the man and replies, "Just what I thought!" The Cowboy enquires, "What you gonna do, Boss?" Joshua Jones looks at his worker, and responds, "I'm gonna tell the other Ranchers what I know!"

# CHAPTER FOUR

*Cowboys Cattle, and Conflict.*

Storm Cloud and his embolden braves raid other herds across the land, stealing more Cattle - and killing more Cowboys. Word quickly spreads to the other Ranches, and the owners rally with a vengeance. They want to end the Indian trouble that vexing them and diminishing their herds. The Ranchers arrange a rendezvous to gather guns and plan their strategy. The Cattle rustling has affected all the Ranchers, big and small, all the owners fear for their operation and lifework. Everyone gathers at one large spread, the **Circle T Ranch**. The owner, big Bart Payton, stirs up the ranchers, Cowboys, and townsfolk, to take action and fight the Indians! The assembled crowd become agitated, raising fists and guns in the air - itching to serve some Wild West justice. Some folk yell out in anger, "Kill the Indians!", "Make the Redskins Suffer!" Amid the heightened excitement, Joshua Jones steps up beside Bart Payton and requests to address the crowd. Bart steps aside and Joshua looks out over the people, and remarks, "NOW, HOLD ON! - I've talked with the Indians and it's not them!" A townsman calls out, "What do you mean it's not them (Points to Cody) Your own man, Cody, said it was Indians that stole the herd and killed Jesse!" The crowd becomes agitated at hearing his words. Joshua raises his arms and motions the group to simmer down. When they quiet some, Joshua continues, "The Indians that attacked my herd and men were led by a young hothead brave called Storm Cloud!" People in the large crowd begin to repeat the name since no one has heard the name before. Joshua gazes at the people and remarks, "The Indian Tribes we know had nothing to do with this. Storm Cloud and his braves are rogue warriors operating on their own! They're the ones we're after!" Someone yells out from the back, "The only good Indian is a dead

Indian!" Joshua fumes at the wicked remark and yells out, "Who said that! Show yourself - Who said such a vile thing?" Everyone in the crowd glances around at each other, and a large man with wild hair and scruffy beard steps through the crowd to stand in front of Joshua. The man looks at those standing around him and remarks, "I was a Scout for the Calvary during the Indian Uprisings! (Scans about) I can tell you all - I saw things that'd make you skin crawl. (Stares at Joshua) Atrocities done by Indians!" The man's words stirs up the crowd again. Joshua puts his hand up to get everyone's attention, and he comments, "The Uprisings were bad times for everyone. Both White Men and Indians did terrible things (looks over crowd) No one's innocent!" A Rancher named, Philip Struthers, near the front of the crowd raises his voice, "What you gonna do, Joshua - keep letting them steal your Cattle and kill your men? (Pause) May be you can afford to loose more, but not me - I run a small operation!" The crowd responds to the Rancher's words with renewed vengeance. Big Bart Payton steps up, lifts his arms to address the people, "You heard from Joshua Jones, and you heard from Phil Struthers, - we got a choice to make here tonight. Do we hunt down this Storm Cloud varmint, or do we just go home?" The people glance each other and some individuals call out, "Hunt 'em down!", "Go after Storm Cloud!" Mr. Payton puts up his hand and sets things clear, "Everyone understand - we leave the Indian Tribes around us alone, and we chase down this rogue warrior, Storm Cloud. Agreed?" The crowd erupts with approval and consent! Bart Payton announces, "Okay folks, for those who don't have stomach for it, you can go home - for everyone else - us Ranchers will join forces to put an end to Storm Cloud and his cattle stealing braves!" The crowd parts with some head for horses and buckboards to go back home, while many others remain at the Circle T Ranch, ready to ride and fight.

# CHAPTER FIVE

## *A New Bloodthirsty Chief*

Disenchanted young braves from many tribes begin to rally to Storm Cloud as a new upcoming Chief. Someone who is not afraid of the White man. These young braves crave the action and wildness found with Storm Cloud's raids and attacks on the Ranches in the territory. The young Indian warriors seek a leadership that reflects their own attitude - to make the Indians mighty again - and take control of the lands and strike fear into the hearts of the Paleface. There are many braves gathered from different Tribes, - Sioux, Cheyenne, Crow, Blackfoot, Arapaho, Ute, and Shoshone. The mix of braves from different backgrounds presents a problem; - soon, there are quarrels and disputes between the various young bucks. Bravado and male ego can be a problem with any large group of young men - no matter what the race or people. Young hot heads are simply that - young hot heads. Storm Cloud has his own internal problems due to the number of rowdy quarrelsome braves, that have joined his growing number of warriors. A few of these rogue braves secretly plan their takeover of leadership with the defeat and removal of Storm Cloud. The new influx of warlike braves and competing personalities makes for a turbulent mix of troops. These young Indian braves all want to fight the White Man, and many are willing to fight each other. Storm Cloud has a couple of braves that he can rely on to support his leadership, two young warriors that have been with him from the beginning - "Grey Wolf" and "Running Elk". Both young braves are skilled warriors, fierce fighters, and strong physically and mentally. Both are determined to stay loyal to Storm Cloud as the self-appointed Indian Chief.

* * *

News of Storm Cloud's growing power spreads to the different Indian Tribes. The various Chiefs and Tribal Elders are greatly concerned at the exodus of their young braves. These fledgling warriors are without any real wisdom, just young men hungry to taste action and adventure. These inexperienced young bloods are ripe for Storm Cloud's control, and easily swayed by the young Chief's rant against the White Man, and his promise to make Indians great once again. Back in the various Tribal villages and Camps; mothers, fathers, grandparents and siblings, fret over the departure of the young men, many just in their late teens and early twenties. The Indian families know their sons are too young to die, and the parents are keenly aware of Storm Cloud's intention to lead their young men into a needless and pointless War - where many will be killed!

# CHAPTER SIX

## *Storm Cloud's War Camp*

Deep in a remote section of Indian lands, far away from the White Man, Storm Cloud has set up his War Party Camp. The rock terrain limits access in and out, thus, providing greater protection for the large number of tepees and canvass shelters set up. Storm Cloud's fighters number nine hundred, strong young braves who have joined his cause and quest for power. The braves bring their weapons and youthful courage, having turned their backs on Tribe, leaders, and family. Storm Cloud makes sure there is plenty of food, water, and Whiskey. After all, with so many young warriors, there needs to be plenty of food and drink. When they're not eating or sleeping, many of the young bucks engage in weapon practice, contests, and wrestling matches. Most of the braves want to show off their warrior skills, physical strength, and fighting ability. At times, the wrestling contests and challenges turn ugly, as the young participants become seized with immature emotion and anger. Even though, the Indian braves have gathered in one place, under a common cause to fight the White Man; it's clearly obvious, the Camp is unofficially divided into different groups, each group made up of Indians associated with specific Tribes. Keeping his War Party cohesive weighs heavy on Storm Cloud's mind. If his warriors cannot stay united, and eventually divide into separate groups, his goal to wage War on the Paleface becomes threatened. That's why Storm Cloud gives his braves plenty of food, drink, and lots of Whiskey, to keep them happy. While his warriors are preoccupied, the rogue Chief and his lieutenants plan out their next big Raid.

As Grey Wolf, Running Elk, and Storm Cloud talk privately in the leader's tepee, Grey Wolf comments, "Our warriors grow restless.

They want to ride and fight as Indian braves of old." Running Elk remarks, "The Indian Uprisings are in the past. Our young warriors crave fresh battles!" Storm Cloud listens to his two close friends, then responds, "Attacks must be carefully planned - the White Men have many guns, and will be on their guard. (Pause) We must attack somewhere they will not expect - somewhere they won't be ready!" The two Lieutenants nod their support. The brash young Chief grins and remarks, "I have just the place to lead our warriors to attack! A White Man target soft and vulnerable. Our War Party will strike fear into the hearts of many Paleface!" Grey Wolf and Running Elk smile at their Chief's plans for further attacks.

That evening, a large bonfire lights up the night sky, as hundreds of braves SHOUT and STOMP around the dancing flames shooting high in the air. The young men are liquored up from all the Whiskey supplied by their young Chief. Previously, Storm Cloud and a small War Party, met with Badger and Grit at an undisclosed location. Storm Cloud had sent two braves with a message that he wanted a lot more Whiskey. At the secret meeting in the wilderness, the young Chief gives the Traders bags of gold in exchange for a number of Whiskey barrels - enough Whiskey to keep his braves happy. The band of Indians brought long poles and thick fabric to create travos to cart the barrels back to Camp. Once there, the barrels are stored in a designated tepee, where posted warriors guard and watch over the Whiskey supply. From this large storage of alcohol, Storm Cloud gives plenty of Whiskey to his braves. All liquored up, these braves YELL, SCREAM, and STOMP the ground around the bonfire. Storm Cloud wants the young men to be full of "liquid courage" before he sends them out for another attack. Filled with booze and bravado, Storm Cloud knows his young warriors will not fear any bullet from the White Man's gun. The Chief smirks with satisfaction as he hears the drunken braves fill the air with RIFLE FIRE, YELLS and WAR CRIES! Grey Wolf and Running Elk join alongside Storm Cloud, and the three rogue leaders contently watch the horde of young warriors party wildly - they're prepared and primed to go out and fight!

# CHAPTER SEVEN

## *The Ranchers' Revenge*

Now, that those not lending their guns have left the Circle T; the Ranchers, Cowboys, Farmers, and Townsfolk, who remain begin to get antsy. The gathered throng vent aloud their anger and frustration, and raise pistols, shotguns, and Winchesters in the air, everyone itching to go after Storm Cloud and his warriors. Big Bart Payton ascends the house veranda and looks over the people. He lifts his rifle and loudly declares, "We gonna make 'em pay - and put a stop to this. NO MORE STOLEN CATTLE!" The crowd gives boisterous CHEERS! Bart Payton points over to Joshua Jones, and remarks, "Are you riding with us?" Joshua Jones gives firm eye contact to the big man, and replies, "Bart. You've known me a long time. My word is my bond! (Nods) You got my gun and the guns of my men, right alongside yours!" Bart Payton smiles and extends his arm, and Joshua Jones steps up and shakes hand. The gesture by the two top Ranchers gives a show of solidarity that helps to unite and motivate the crowd even more. All the people show their approval by letting out loud SHOUTS!

Joshua Jones has 45 Cowboys with him, Bart Payton's Ranch Hands are 40, and the rest of the "Rustlers Posse" is made up of the other Ranchers, Hired Hands, some Farmers, and Townsfolk. Altogether, those going after Storm Cloud are 200 strong. Every person carries a firearm and knows how to shoot, and many of the Cowboys holster 2 pistols, plus their rifle. Bart Payton smiles as he views the attack force - Storm Cloud will face many guns. The big ranch owner calls out over the crowd, "Grab a place to sleep in barns and bunkhouses. We ride out at dawn!" The people disband and make way to the barns and bunkhouses on the Circle T property. Many simply find some dry hay to lay on - and try and get some sleep for the big day ahead.

Bright and early the next morning at dawn, as the morning light crests over the horizon, Bart Payton and Joshua Jones are in the saddle, ready to ride. They are soon surrounded by their Cowboys. The veteran ranchers watch as the volunteers get awake and begin to muster in the large open barnyard. The people are a mixed bag - townsfolk with pistols in rumpled clothes from sleeping in the hay, simple farmers holding shotguns, and Hired Hands carrying rifles. Everyone mounts up on horseback. There's an uneasy quiet as the 200 souls wait and watch for Bart and Joshua's lead. The two old ranchers looks around at their armed Posse and Bart eyes Joshua, "Appears they're ready." Joshua reins his horse around in a tight circle to scan the group, and remarks, "Time to hunt down the renegade Storm Cloud! There'll be lots of fighting and shooting (Scan around) Some of us may get wounded - Some of us may die! (Pause) No matter what - Storm Cloud must be dealt with!" The crowd CHEERS! Joshua looks at Bart and the big man YELLS OUT, "Let's Ride!" With the order given, the armed riders move their horses. The Posse launches out toward distant Indian lands, where reports say Storm Cloud and his braves have a Hideout.

The Posse rides over the Circle T Ranch, the Double J Ranch and other spreads, before going deep into the wilderness close to Indian territory. The men and horses wind their way through the tundra shrubs, stubby trees, tall grass, and rocky outcrops. Unbeknown to Joshua and Bart, Storm Cloud has lookouts posted throughout the frontier Indian lands to keep their eyes open for any Paleface. The large Rancher Posse are quite noticeable, and soon the Indian sentries catch sight of the intruders, and make haste to inform their Chief. In the hidden Camp, Storm Cloud and his Lieutenants are planning strategy, when two Indian sentries ride into Camp and go directly to their Chief. The faces on the sentries tell Storm Cloud and the other two that something is wrong. The braves approach and one brave exclaims, "Many Paleface riders have entered our lands!" The young Chief glances at his lieutenants, then looks at the two sentries and asks, "How many?" The other brave replies, "Very many horses - over one hundred - maybe more!" The two braves keep their gaze on Storm Cloud as he ponders the new information. The young Chief looks out over his warriors and declares, "These are our lands. We know where to attack the Paleface!" The Rogue Chief glances at Grey Wolf and Running Elk, and orders,

"Get our Warriors ready. We attack the White Man!" Grey Wolf and Running Elk nod, and swiftly leave to alert the braves and assemble the War Party. In minutes, the entire War Party are mounted with rifles, spears, tomahawks, bows and arrows. The young braves are excited and energized to go into Battle. Storm Cloud rides his spotted horse into their midst, and yells, "WE ATTACK THE PALEFACE!" The War Party fills the air with loud WAR CRIES, SHOUTS, and BATTLE CRIES! Storm Cloud waves his arm and the mass of Indian warriors bolt their horses forward, charging out of Camp to fight their foe. The young Chief leads his warriors through trails known only to Territory Indians. These routes are shortcuts that give Storm Cloud and the War Party the time and advantage to set up traps to ambush the Rancher Posse. The rogue Chief divides the War Party into three groups, each group will strike from a hidden location. The Rancher Posse will be caught off-guard and be vulnerable. As the Warriors quietly wait, Indian scouts alert the Chief and leaders that the Paleface riders are coming.

# CHAPTER EIGHT

## *Hot Lead and Sharp Arrows*

Bart Payton and Joshua Jones ride at the front of the Posse. The men look here and there, keeping their eyes peeled, as they cover ground. To their knowledge, Storm Cloud's Camp is deep in Indian lands, there's a way to go, so the group ride with a relaxed attitude. The Posse group eventually approach an large open area leading to four separate Canyons. Bart Payton lifts up his arm to signal the riders to stop. He turns to Joshua and remarks, "Four paths ahead - which one do you think we should take?" Joshua stares a bit at what's out front, then he relies, "The two passages on the right lead deeper into Indian lands. The two on the left will take riders toward the grasslands." Big Bart Payton nods, and comments, "We will take the two on the right - toward Indian lands!" The man turns around to see those gathered behind, then he waves his arm forward and calls out, "Move out to the right!" The two Ranchers steer their horses toward the two Canyon openings on the right. As the Rancher Posse reach the middle of the open ground that lays before the canyons - INDIAN WAR CRIES - fill the air! War Party braves pour out of two Canyons in front of them, shooting their rifles and arrows at the men caught in the open ground with nothing to hide behind. Suddenly, another bunch of War Party Braves attack from the rear where the Posse just traveled through. Arrows and bullets fly at the Posse from three separate directions, the Ranchers, Cowboys, Farmers, and Townsfolk, are caught in the open with no protection. Joshua yells out, "Shoot your rifles. They're too far for pistols." There's both commotion and confusion, as the Posse fire their guns while their horses jostle and move about. Shooting stationary targets from horseback is one thing, but, shooting at moving targets while your horse is spooked and moving around, is a very difficult thing! Many of the bullets fired by the Posse are wild and don't find their mark. Some of the Cowboys shoot their rifles with deadly accuracy, killing attacking braves in their sights. Joshua and Bart fire their Winchesters at the oncoming braves. The air is full of bullets and arrows. Joshua raises his rifle, fires and shoots a warrior off his horse. Joshua turns his head toward his old friend, and is horrified to see two arrows strike deep into Bart Payton's chest. The big Rancher slumps forward and falls off his horse to lands in the dirt. THUD! Joshua jumps off his horse and crouches down close to his friend, he stares at the two arrow shafts protruding from the chest, blood streams from the wounds. He tries to lift Bart's head and the man groans in agony, "OOOHHH!" Joshua realizes there's nothing he can do for his friend. As Joshua looks at Bart's face, the wounded man lets out his last breath and dies with his eyes still open. Joshua places his fingertips on Bart's face and closes the eyelids. He looks at his dead friend, then gets to his feet, lifts up the Winchester and begins firing. The gunfire is intense as the Indians and the Ranchers shoot at each other. Grey gun smoke lingers in the air. The bodies of Indians and Cowboys lay in the dust. In the thick of the action, with arrows and bullets flying around, Joshua sizes up the situation and knows the Posse must make a break, and charge in one direction. He looks about and thinks - which direction? Joshua calls out to Cody, "Head back the way we came! Fight our way through!" Cody nods and quickly passes the message. Quickly, the Posse turn their guns and horses to confront the Indians at the rear. Joshua, Cody and the others, blast their rifles and pistols at the braves in their path. A barrage of hot lead clears the way as the braves are wounded, killed, or scared off. The Rancher Posse ride hard and put ground between them and Storm Cloud's War Party in pursuit. The Posse repeatedly fire at the Indians giving chase - and soon, the Indian Warriors stop chasing. The ambush cost many lives for both Indian and Ranchers. The open ground where the attack took place is littered with scores of dead bodies. The majority of those who died are young Indian braves, warriors filled with youthful courage, yet gravely inexperienced with warfare and the reality of death. Storm Cloud looks at his slain braves as he rides his horse across the ground. He realizes the ambush did not have the devastation he envisioned. As his War Party retrieve the deceased braves for transport to Camp, Storm Cloud knows there will be other young braves that will join to replenish his fighters. The War Party slowly ride back toward Camp, many of the horses carrying their rider, as well as the dead body of a young Indian brave.

The Posse ride hard and long, and only ease up when they reach familiar territory. Of the 200 Posse members - those returning number 140 riders. Bart Payton and the other dead men lay on the ground in Indian Territory. There will be no customary wake, funeral, or cemetery burial. The wilderness can be a harsh cruel place. Many of the Posse are unsettled because they know their dead friends will be found by the coyotes and vultures. Most of the Posse trip back to the Circle T Ranch is quiet with little conversation, the survivors left in silent reflection. The group reach the Circle T Ranch property, and stop their horses outside the large main house. Joshua lifts his eyes to the home where his old friend, Bart Payton lived. His heart is sad. Joshua dismounts and walks up the veranda steps, looks out over the remaining Posse riders, and remarks, "We lost a lot of people today - good friends and neighbours!" The Posse members exchange eye contact with each other. Joshua comments, "We must help take care of the widows and children of the men who were killed. They will need our help!" Everyone nods agreement. Joshua Jones steps off the veranda to stand with the group, and remarks, "We did our part - Storm Cloud has fewer braves (Pause) Mark my word - Storm Cloud will be stopped!" The Posse voice their support! Joshua begins to walk among the Posse to shake hands and express his gratitude for their involvement. The men slowly leave in small groups, heading back to their homes, farms, and ranches. As Joshua watches the people ride out from the Circle T, Cody approaches his Boss and remarks, "Sorry about your friend, Bart!" Joshua turns his attention to Cody, puts his hand on Cody's shoulder and replies, "He was a good man and a good friend. We both started our ranches at the same time. (Pause) Gonna miss the big guy!" He looks at Cody and comments, "Let's go home (grins) We got a ranch to run!" Cody replies, "You got it Boss! The Double J is our home!" The two men mount their horses. It's late in the evening when Joshua Jones, Cody, and the Double J Cowboys ride out, leaving the Circle T Ranch behind them.

# CHAPTER NINE

## *Burning Ranches to the Ground*

The War Party ride hard over pastureland toward the Ranch house and barns nestled by the river. The spread is known as the "Miller Creek Ranch". Storm Cloud and his braves descend with YELLS and WAR CRIES! The Cowboys are busy branding livestock near the pens, and caught off guard. Surprised and alarmed, the Ranch Hands jump into action and draw their guns to shoot at the attacking Indians. The War Party let loose a stream of fire arrows that hit the Ranch house, Bunkhouse, and Barns. The dry wood instantly ignites and the flames quickly spread to cover the roofs and walls. Soon, all the buildings are ablaze with flames shooting up high. The air begins to get thick with smoke, making it difficult for the Cowboys to aim and shoot the attackers. The smoke makes the men cough and squint their eyes, as fire rages all around them. They're caught in the middle of the burning wooden structures. Boxed in by flames on three sides, the Cowboys try to escape by fighting their way through the one clear side. Storm Cloud sits on his horse at a distance, and watches his braves shower the Ranch Hands with arrows and bullets. Like shooting fish in a barrel - the Cowboys are trapped with searing hot flames on three sides - and Indians attacking on the other side. Many of the Cowboys are killed and lay in the dirt, their dead bodies full of arrows like a pin cushion. The surviving Cowboys hunker down by a pile of rocks that give only sparse cover. There's a lull in the fighting and the Ranch Hands catch their breath and tend to their wounds. Crouched behind the shallow rock pile, the Cowboys raise their heads to check what's happening. The men see different groups of Indians in War Paint surrounding them. The four Cowboys realize they don't stand a chance. The river on the other side of the burning buildings is their only option. The men decide to make a break for it and dash through the flames and burning structures, running hard for the river. The braves see the escaping Cowboys and fire their arrows and bullets - a group of warriors bolt their horse to give chase - YELLING and SCREAMING! The Ranch Hands rush past the flames, leaping over the burning debris of the collapsed house, heading toward the deep river. Right on their heels, the pursuing Warriors pull back their bows to shoot their arrows and fire their rifles. The four Cowboys see the open water and hope rises, they're going to jump into the river where the Indian riders and horses cannot follow. As they get close near the river bank, three Cowboys drop to the ground - with arrows and bullets in the back. The lone Cowboy runs with all his might and dives into the water to disappear beneath the surface. The Warriors chasing him reach the river bank and scan the water for any sign of the White Man. The surviving Cowboy is a good swimmer, and swims underwater far way from the river bank, out into the deep water. He comes up to the surface to get air, and quickly looks at the shore. The Indians that gave chase, sit on horseback by the river's edge - the river is too deep for their horses to follow. The braves see the Cowboy and shoot arrows and fire their rifles at him. He ducks under the water and swims for the riverbank on the other side, where he will be safe. The man comes up to the surface near the riverbank, and climbs up on grass and dirt, and sprawls out panting for air. He lifts his head to see Storm Cloud and his War Party ride away from burning ruins. The Miller Creek Ranch, is a smouldering rubble of blacken charred timber, where once stood a Ranch House, Bunkhouse, and two Cattle Barns. The lone Cowboy stands to his feet and heads off toward the nearest Ranch, where he will tell others of the latest attack, how Storm Cloud and his rogue warriors killed the Ranch Hands, and burned down the Miller Creek Ranch!

# CHAPTER TEN

## *The Soft Vulnerable Target*

The wind gently blows across the Plains bending the tall grass, making the blades of grass dance and sway in the breeze. The sun shines bright in the sky above, the temperature is ever so pleasant. Voices fill the air with laughter and frolic, as the children play outdoors as they gleefully chase each other in a game of tag. Their big red Prairie School House sits amid a grove of oak and elm trees. All around the wood building, the school children enjoy their time of Recess, thoroughly taking advantage of being outside before the Bell rings calling all the students inside for class. Miss Rachel, the School Teacher, stands on the steps of the building's entrance, and chuckles as she watches the energetic play of the young ones. She is an attractive young lady, with a sweet smile and flowing locks of auburn hair going past her shoulder. Miss Rachel arrived two years ago from Boston, out East, where she earned her Diploma in Teaching. The young lady had always dreamed of teaching out West, and applied to be the local School Mistress for Oak Grove Primary School located in the Great Plains. In her mind, there's no more wonderful place to be teaching her children at the big red School House. Miss Rachel looks up at the sun shining high, and decides it is time to commence studies, and lifts her hand that grips the bell's wooden handle. Back and forth she swings her arm, and rings the shiny brass bell, the bright clear sound carries far and wide. The children stop their outdoor fun time, and some of the kids moan at the loss of their playtime. The boys and girls line up in an orderly fashion and begin to file up the front steps and into the building. Miss Rachel observes as she stands to the side. As the last student passes through the doorway, Miss Rachel looks to check if any student is still outside. Seeing no one is around, she enters and closes the School's front door.

The muffled noise of students getting seated and opening the wooden tops of their desks can be heard outside. The next session of schooling involves Singing, an activity that both students and Miss Rachel delight in. The young School Teacher sits down at the upright piano and opens the Sheet Music for the popular Hymn by the blind songwriter, Fanny Crosby - "Blessed Assurance". As the keys of the piano sound out the music, Miss Rachel and her students sing out the lyrics "Blessed Assurance, Jesus is Mine."

## SUDDENLY - INDIAN WAR CRIES!

All the children become alarmed and scared. Miss Rachel quickly leaves the piano to look out the window - she freezes with fright! Fearsome Indian warriors in War Paint on horseback are riding around the School House - YELLING, SHOUTING, and SCREAMING! The children rush to the windows to look out. Many burst into tears and start to cry aloud. Some little girls and boys run to cling to Miss Rachel's frilly calico dress. The young lady glances down at the young ones hugging tightly to her. She puts her hand on their heads to try and calm their little hearts. The War Party braves are loud and scary, as they ride circles around the big wood structure. The braves hold up their rifles, spears and bows, letting out blood-cuddling SCREAMS and WAR CRIES! Inside the one room School House, all the children are crying and petrified. Their young eyes look to their Teacher for help. Miss Rachel's heart is deeply moved at seeing her students griped with such fear. She lifts her gaze out the glass window to see a spotted horse with a fierce young warrior in an Chief's War Bonnet ride into her sight. The Indian braves all stop riding at their Chief's arrival. Storm Cloud looks at Miss Rachel standing at the window with little children clinging tightly to her. The rogue Chief sneers and points his War Lance at the building. Immediately several braves jump off their horses and bust through the door to stand menacingly in the doorway. All the children rush to gather around their Teacher. Miss Rachel reaches out her arms to off some form of protection to cover the youngsters. She looks at the warriors holding their weapons, inside her soul, she trembles with fear and dread. The braves walk to the front of the large open classroom, sending any remaining students to flee to the Teacher's side. The Warriors slowly walk toward the young lady and the students gathered around her, much like tiny chicks gathered around a mother hen. Instinctively, Miss Rachel and her students back away from the approaching braves. The Teacher and children continue to back away until they're eventually at the front entrance of the School House. The Warriors inside, keep stepping closer and closer, and Miss Rachel and the young children back out of the entrance, and are now outside. The warriors keep walking until they fill the front entrance, blocking any way to go inside. Miss Rachel scans about, the school children are crying and sobbing. More Indian braves close in, and move toward her and the students, driving them further away from the red School House, and toward the cluster of Oak trees. Once Miss Rachel and the children reach the trees, the Warriors stop their approach and return to mount up on their horses. By now, a few small fires are burning on the ground around the building. Storm Cloud eyes the Teacher and cowering children, then waves his arm as he shouts, "BURN IT DOWN!" The War Party dip their arrows to catch fire - then the braves pull back their bows and shoot the burning arrows at the big red School House. The fire brands sink into the wooden walls, roof, and door of the School House. The wooden structure quickly catches fire and the flames rapidly spread across the entire building. In a matter of minutes, the School House is a raging inferno as flames consumes the roof, walls, floor, and wooden desks inside. The air is filled with the sound of crackling flames and falling timber, as the building collapses on itself. Black smoke rises high into the sky, letting others know far away know that there's a big fire.

As Miss Rachel and the crying children sadly watch their School House burn to the ground, Storm Cloud rides his horse to within a few paces of them. Storm Cloud looks fierce and scary in his War Paint. The young Chief looks into Miss Rachel's eyes with a cold firm stare, and holds his gaze for a couple minutes. The young School Teacher from Boston has never been so close to a real live Indian before, much less an actual War Chief. Storm Cloud glances over at his warriors who are on their mounts watching the big fire. He reins his horse away from Miss Rachel and the children, and bolts his horse forward to joins fighters. Storm Cloud lifts high the War Lance and cries out, "We ride to Camp!" The horde of Indian warriors respond the their Chief's order, and swiftly ride away - leaving behind a smouldering black rubble of charred lumber. Miss Rachel and the children watch as the Indians ride further away and disappear out of sight. In her heart, Miss Rachel is overjoyed that none of her precious children were killed, however, she's greatly saddened at the loss of their School House.

Now that the fearsome Indian warriors are gone, some children begin to ask questions, "Miss Rachel, what will we do?", a few little ones cry out, "I'm scared! I want my Mommy." The young woman attempts to calm the youngsters. The School Teacher looks at the faces of her young students and remarks in a confident comforting tone, "We will start walking toward town." The group of bewildered youngsters and a shaken Miss Rachel begin to head toward Town, located 3 miles in the distance. With the demolished School House behind them, the group walk on the dusty road toward Town, when a large group of riders and people in wagons approach them. Reaching close, one of the townsmen on horseback declares, "Everyone in town saw the smoke. We rushed here as soon as we could!" A concerned lady in a buckboard asks, "What happened?" Miss Rachel looks at the faces of the people and replies, "Indians. Indians in War Paint burnt down our School House!" Miss Rachel notices their frightened reaction. The folks are visibly alarmed and scared that warlike Indian braves carried out a Raid so close to town.

# CHAPTER ELEVEN

## *Local Meetings and Fearful People*

Returning to their hidden Camp in the Rock Canyons of Indian Territory, Storm Cloud and the War Party feel bold and victorious. Their attacks on the numerous Ranches, Farms, and now, the big red School House, has sent fear into the hearts of the settlers and townsfolk on the Plains. It seems no where is safe from attacks by Storm Cloud and his rogue warriors. People in communities large and small, gather at town meetings to discuss the growing threat facing everyone. The meetings are boisterous and heated as individuals and various groups argue and yell at each other about what to do. Families with little children are concerned, local farmers and ranchers fear for their herds and homesteads, townsfolk and merchants fear that Storm Cloud and his horde of wild warriors will attack their communities - the very place they work and sleep. A shroud of dread has settled over all the people across the Plains.

In the Town Meeting of JUNIPER JUNCTION, the local farmers, settlers and merchants discuss the growing danger of Indian Attacks. The meeting is lively and peppered with lots of questions - and few answers. One farmer, "Ezekiel Vanderklap" stands up in the gathering and raises the question, "What don't we call in the Calvary? (Looks around room) The soldiers will put a stop to it!" The entire crowd reacts to Ezekiel's question, the men and women call out, "Yes! Get the Army!", "Ezekiel's right! Call in the soldiers!" The farmer's question hits upon what many have thought, and unlocks a flood of emotion. The community leaders try to restore order. The Mayor raises his hands to quiet the people down, and remarks, "Now calm down! Everybody just calm down!" The townsfolk, ranchers, and farmers, begin to settle down and wait to hear out their Mayor. The portly man stands to his feet and gazes around the packed room, and comments, "The reason why we cannot call in the Calvary is - the Government must honour the Peace Treaty with the different Tribes." The Mayor looks across the peoples' faces, and continues, "The Indian Tribes are not at War with us! These Attacks are done by a rogue Chief and his young warriors! As far as the Government is concerned - the Tribes have kept the Treaty!" A lady holding her one year old baby, stands up and tearfully asks, "If the Army won't help us - What are we to do? (Scans room) What about our children?" The room erupts with loud comments, shouts and calls, the community leaders exchange perplexed glances with the Mayor. The man lifts his arms to quiet the room again. As the folks simmer down and await his words, the Mayor remarks, "Our town has enough men and rifles. We will establish Town Guards, day and night. If there's any attack (draws his pistol) we'll be ready!" Heads across the room nod, and the people are appeased with the Mayor's solution. The people realize if they stand together, there'll be safety in numbers. After all, that's the way it was with the big Wagon Trains that came across the Great Plains that brought the settlers, farmers and ranchers. The early pioneers faced hostile Indians and cruel bandits, and to survive, they stood together and fought as one. The people of Juniper Junction will do the same - that's the way of the Wild West!

# CHAPTER TWELVE

## *The Shoshone Indian Village*

The Shoshone Village stirs at the news of exploits by Storm Cloud and his growing force of rogue warriors. Like the other Tribal Villages across the Plains, young Shoshone braves have left to join Storm Cloud's War Party. Families with sons gone, are grief stricken with emotion, and plead with Buffalo Sky and their Elders to do something. A Tribal Council is called!

The leading Warriors gather in the large central tepee for Tribal Council with Chief Buffalo Sky and the Elders. Bear Claw, Eagle Feather, Two Knives, Otter, and Yuji, sit in the Council Circle. Other warriors are also present, the big tepee filled to capacity, while many Shoshone braves are gathered outside. As the drums and chanting stop, Chief Buffalo Sky lifts his arm to signal and quiet all conversation. He speaks, "My Shoshone brothers - many have heard of the terrible things being done by this wild brave called Storm Cloud! (Heads nod) We know young braves from many different Tribes have run off to join his War Party. (Pause) If Storm Cloud is not stopped - he will start a big War with the White Man - people who have become our friends. (Buffalo Sky Stands up) Many young Indian braves will be killed, and many White people will die - We must prevent this from happening!" The entire large tepee is abuzz with support. Bear Claw lifts his arm to speak - and the tepee becomes quiet. The seasoned warrior remarks, "Our Ninjans and Warriors can stop Storm Cloud! We will find his secret Camp and remove this arrogant troublesome Chief!" Buffalo Sky and the Elders confer, then give their approval. Buffalo Sky points his hand to Yuji and Otter, and comments, "Yuji and Otter will lead our Shoshone Ninjans. (Points) Bear Claw, Eagle

Feather, and Two Knives, will lead our Warriors!" The entire assembly voice their approval with traditional Shoshone SHOUTS and WAR CRIES! Chief Buffalo Sky and the Elders stand to their feet, and Buffalo Sky waves his arm toward the leading Warriors, Yuji and Otter, and remarks, "Be Strong. Fight well. Capture Storm Cloud!" Everyone in the central tepee stands to their feet to give their support. Yuji and Otter, look at Bear Claw, Eagle Feather, and Two Knives - all five nod and lift high their weapons as a rally sign! The Chief, the Elders, and the assembled warriors - fill the large tepee with SHOUTS, YELLS, and BATTLE CRIES!

The Shoshone braves who gathered for Tribal Council disperse to their own tepees, while Chief Buffalo Sky and the Elders remain at the Council Fire. Bear Claw, Eagle Feather, Two Knives exit along with Yuji and Otter. Bear Claw looks at his fellow warriors and comments, "We will meet at my tepee to plan." The others nod agreement and the five make their way past village tepees, until they arrive at Bear Claw's home. Bear Claw lifts the buckskin flap and bids everyone go inside. Once everyone has entered, Bear Claw closes the entrance flap and walks over to sit on the tepee floor cross-legged like the others. Bear Claw's wife, "Summer Rain", has placed bannock, fruits, and strips of dried venison, before the tepee guests. Bear Claw looks at the men and gestures with a smile, "Eat my friends. Our talk may be long." Eagle Feather, Two Knives, Yuji, and Otter begin to eat to appease their appetites. Bear Claw is happy his guests like the staples that has been supplied. As the men sit together and eat the food items, Two Knives offers a suggestion, "At sunrise, I will take a brave and go ahead to search for Storm Cloud's Camp." Yuji remarks, "When we reach the spot you find, the Ninjans will set up explosions to startle his warriors. (Eyes others) We can attack Storm Cloud in the confusion!" Bear Claw looks at Yuji and remarks, "Two Knives, Eagle Feather, and myself will overpower those close by him - then, we will take him captive." Otter questions, "You will not kill Storm Cloud?" The seasoned brave gazes at Otter and replies, "We will take him before the Council of Chiefs. He must give account for the  terrible trouble caused between the Indian Tribes and the White Man. (Pause) The Chiefs will decide Storm Cloud's punishment!" Everyone nods at Bear Claw's words - they understand the Tribal wisdom of allowing the Council of Chiefs to decide Storm Cloud's fate!" As the last of the bannock, fruit and venison disappear, Summer Rain graciously brings a second supply for their visitors. Eagle Feather nods to the woman, and comments, "Guests in your tepee are well-cared for!" Summer Rain blushes a bit and responds, "Never have so many of our greatest warriors gathered in our tepee at one time. Our tepee is greatly honoured at your presence." Bear Claw looks at his wife with a smile, and softly touches her arm as she moves by. It's the touch that married couples share when no words are spoken, yet both share the understanding. Bear Claw lets Summer Rain know that he is proud of her and the fine words she has spoken. The men finish the second helping and respectfully sit quiet, awaiting Bear Claw's dismissal for the meeting he called. Two Knives looks at everyone and remarks, "We need our top warriors with us. Five of us will not be enough! Storm Cloud has hundreds in his War Party!" Yuji interjects, "Our Ninjans number 37 - each one better than ten braves!" Bear Claw lifts his hand and comments, "Tomorrow, I will choose warriors from our Camp to join us. (Pause) We will be strong!" The men nod agreement. A few minutes pass, then, Bear Claw looks at the men and remarks, "You have honoured our tepee! Sleep well tonight, my brothers." Eagle Feather, Two Knives, Yuji, and Otter stand to their feet, smile at their hosts, and exit the dwelling. Each man goes home to his own tepee. The time is late in the evening, and the Shoshone Camp lays peaceful and quiet.

The next morning, the Shoshone warriors are assembled, eager and ready for Bear Claw's inspection. Yuji and Otter, with the Shoshone Ninjans, stand off to the side to observe. Bear Claw walks among the Tribe's warriors. He looks at the faces of the braves, and notes how they stand to present themselves. All the Tribe stand around them, the Shoshone villagers are keen to see which ones Bear Claw will select. Chief Buffalo Sky and the Elders are at the central tepee to witness the gathering. As Bear Claw moves among the braves, he puts a hand on the shoulder of those he selects. He remembers that Yuji did the same thing when choosing braves for Ninja training. Bear Claw reasons the same approach will also serve his purpose well. When he finishes identifying the warriors, Bear Claw walks up to Eagle Feather and nods. Eagle Feather lifts his voice loud and clear for all to hear, "The warriors touched on the shoulder will join us to go after Storm Cloud! All other braves will remain in our Camp." The Indian braves not touched, begin to disband and take spots among the Shoshone Villagers. The chosen braves remain standing where they are, awaiting further words of instruction. Two Knives walks over to Eagle Feather and Bear Claw, and the three leaders look out over the selected fighters. Bear Claw steps forward, and remarks, "You have been chosen because I know something of your ability to track, hunt, and fight. You will need to use all your skills to help us capture Storm Cloud!" The selected braves begin to comment and converse with one another. Eagle Feather raises his voice, "Prepare yourself and get your weapons - we leave Camp when the sun is high in the sky." The braves look at the three leaders, then quickly disperse in all directions. Each one heading for his tepee to prepare for the danger ahead.

The noonday sun is high overhead, Bear Claw and Eagle Feather sit on their mounts near the Chief's large central tepee, waiting for the braves to assemble. Previously, Two Knives and another brave left Camp at first light, heading out to scout the location of Storm Cloud's War Camp. As the two leaders watch, various Shoshone braves on horseback with rifles, bows, spears, and tomahawks, gather from across their Tribal Village. Soon, the large group of the selected braves are before the two leaders, alert and ready for the task to hunt down Storm Cloud. As one last brave, who is late, gallops his horse up to join the others, Bear Claw lifts his arm and speaks aloud, "We will ride fast and take Tall Pines Trail to the Painted Rocks." All the braves give acknowledgement. Eagle Feather remarks to the warriors, "Many young braves from different tribes are with Storm Cloud. We might fight our Shoshone braves who have joined this wild Chief." The group of Shoshone warriors exchange eye contact with each other, many nod their heads with understanding. At that moment, Chief Buffalo Sky and the Elders emerge from the tepee, and gaze at their Tribe's warriors. The revered Chief lifts up both arms toward the Shoshone Raiding Party, and declares, "Ride fast. Fight well my Shoshone brothers! Bring us Storm Cloud!" The Shoshone respond with loud SHOUTS, YELLS, and BATTLE CRIES! Bear Claw lifts his arm and waves forward. The mass of armed Shoshone warriors swiftly ride out of Camp, Bear Claw and Eagle Feather leading them in the direction of the Tall Pines Trail, and toward the Painted Rocks. It's been said, Storm Cloud has the War Party Camp hidden deep amid the rock canyons, which makes any approach difficult and dangerous.

# CHAPTER THIRTEEN

## *The Painted Canyons*

Two Knives and his fellow Shoshone warrior travel the windswept Plains, being very careful to be unseen and unheard. The veteran Indian Tracker follows the hoof impressions left by horses belonging to Storm Cloud's War Party. The horse tracks lead Two Knives and his companion right toward the Painted Canyons of Indian lands; a rugged landscape of time-sculpted rock formations, stone towers, and a complex of canyons that seem endless, twisting and turning every which way. Deep in these rock canyons, Storm Cloud has purposely chosen to hide the stolen cattle in an obscure canyon that has a narrow entrance that provides protection and limited access. The canyon's interior opens up to provide plenty of room, enough space for the rustled cattle, and even many hundreds more. War Party braves stand on the rock ledges and formations above, to be lookouts for any intruders, and to guard the prized cattle below. The War Party Camp sits in the open ground that lays before the Canyon entrance. Storm Cloud's Camp which started out as a cluster of tepees and shelters, has now become a wide expanse of tepees, huts, and canvass shelters. The rogue braves that at one-time numbered nine hundred, has now grown to become 1400 warriors. The legend and lore of Storm Cloud has even drawn older mature braves, Indian warriors who believe Storm Cloud will restore the Indian Glory of the distant past.

Two Knives travels with his hand-picked scouting companion, "Mountain Bird", a Shoshone brave of stout heart and strong character, and a brave that knows the wilderness well. Two Knives chose Mountain Bird because he can trust the younger brave's scouting and hunting instincts, having another set of eyes and ears will greatly help to find Storm Cloud's secret War Camp. Having hundreds of warriors can be an advantage in battle; however, covering up the many horse tracks makes it more difficult, if not impossible. Having so many warriors, Storm Cloud feels bold and untouchable, and forgets the basics known by all Indians, that of hiding your horse tracks. It is these very horse tracks that lead Two Knives and Mountain Bird directly to the secret Canyon Hideout.

Two Knives and Mountain Bird ride their horses as close as possible, then dismount and quietly crawl across the top of rocks. They keep their bodies low hugging the rock to be unseen by the Indian sentries. The two Shoshone scouts slowly creep their way to a high elevation that overlooks the War Camp and Canyon with stolen cattle. Two Knives scans the large War Camp with its hundreds of tepees, huts, and shelters. He sees hundreds of armed warriors, a fearsome mass of fighters, now experienced with numerous raids and killings. Mountain Bird nudges Two Knives to get his attention, and the younger brave points to a Tepee with a War Lance planted in the ground out front. Two Knives and Mountain Bird realize the War Lance identifies the tepee belonging to the Chief - Storm Cloud. Two Knives carefully notes the exact location of the rogue Chief's dwelling. Having discovered the secret War Camp and memorized the location of Storm Cloud's tepee, Two Knives and Mountain Bird sneak away slow and cautious, as not to be seen by the posted Indian guards. Crawling back to their horses, the two men quietly lead their horse on foot, softly treading to a safe distance before they mount up and rise away. Two Knives and Mountain Bird ride to meet with Bear Claw, Yuji, and the others, to tell of their important discovery!

CHAPTER FOURTEEN

*Ninjans In the War Camp*

Bear Claw, Eagle Feather, and the Shoshone warriors, along with Yuji, Otter and the Ninjans, ride over the rolling grasslands. On the horizon before them are rock formations that form the edge of the Painted Canyons. As they leave the grassy tundra to draw near the rocks, the group see two riders emerge from the contorted stone landscape heading their way. Bear Claw squints his eyes to focus better, and smiles as he recognizes the rider's form, it's his old friend and fellow warrior, Two Knives. The Shoshone group halt their horses and wait. Two Knives and Mountain Bird quickly reach them and hale their fellow Shoshone braves. Two Knives brings his mount up beside Bear Claw, looks at the leader and remarks, "We found their War Camp (Pause) and Storm Cloud's tepee." Bear Claw looks at Yuji and confidently comments, "The Ninjans will help capture Storm Cloud!" Eagle Feather, Two Knives, and Mountain Bird, nod their heads in agreement. Yuji firmly injects, "Our Shoshone Ninjans will not fail!" Bear Claw announces to the others, "Two Knives will take us to the hidden Camp." The veteran Scout cautions, "We must be very quiet - there are many guards!" Eagle Feather raises the point, "If we divide our forces - only send our Ninjans - there will be no noise!" Bear Claw ponders his old friend's advice and agrees, "Eagle Feather is right. Yuji, Otter and the Ninjans will steal into their Camp to capture Storm Cloud. Our warriors will remain at a distance - ready for battle if needed." All the Leaders like the strategy and show support. Bear Claw lifts up his arm for all the Shoshone Raiding Party to hear his orders, "Our leaders and the Ninjans will secretly enter the Camp to capture our prey! The rest of you will hide nearby - ready to be called if needed." Having given his instruction, Bear Claw waves his arm, and the Shoshone braves ride forward to enter the contorted rock formations that lead into the Painted Canyons.

Bear Claw and the braves follow Two Knives as he leads them through the large rock clusters, ridges, and stone towers. The rugged surroundings are made of contorted stone forms shaped by wind and time. The Shoshone Raiding Party wind their way through the rocky landscape with Two Knives and Mountain Bird pointing the way. After considerable travel, the group get within distance of the Painted Canyons, a twisting meandering complex of small and large Canyons. Some Canyons are long winding channels that result in dead ends, while many Canyons lead to yet other Canyons, which crisscross and inter-connect, creating a bewildering array of corridors, hollows, and open ground. All the while, travellers are hemmed in by towering rock walls. The Painted Canyons got their name eons ago because the Canyon walls feature stone layers of various colour - as if an Artist had painted the Canyon walls with lines of different colour. The Painted Canyons are beautiful for the eye to behold, but now, have become deadly since Storm Cloud and his renegades have put their War Camp here.

The Shoshone Warriors reach where Two Knives informs Bear Claw, "This is the place to stop." Bear Claw turns about to tell the others, "The Leaders and Ninjans will go on foot. The rest of you stay with our horses. (Pause) Keep your weapons ready to fight if we call." Yuji, Otter, and the Ninjans dismount, and Bear Claw, Eagle Feather, and Two Knives do the same. Mountain Bird remains behind to lead the others if they're called to fight. As the first group stand on the ground, Bear Claw motions to Two Knives, "Lead the way my brother." The veteran hunter and tracker leads with the others following. Yuji, Otter and the Ninjans bear assorted lethal weapons - Katana and Ninjato swords, Tomahawks, Knives, Shuriken throwing stars, sharp Chain Darts, deadly Blowpipes, various Bombs, and pouches with Powders and Poisons. The Shoshone Force move to the perimeter of the War Camp, and Two Knives signals stop. The Scout points to an upper elevation and motions to climb upward. Everyone carefully climbs up to reach the high vantage point. The elevated position allows them to see the entire War Camp while remaining unseen by the posted sentries. Two Knives with his expert wilderness skills, has found the right spot that gives perfect line-of-sight The group can conduct their important Raid from this spot. As the Shoshone observe the large War Camp spread out before them, Two Knives directs Bear Claw and Yuji's attention to the Tepee with the War Lance at the entrance. Bear Claw and Yuji focus on the tepee's position, committing its location to memory. The Raiding Party lay flat on the rock surface, being mindful to keep a low profile. The afternoon sun is sinking in the sky, and in few couple hours, it will be sunset. The Leaders agree the Raid will be after sunset when light is fading. The Leaders and the Ninjan warriors patiently wait. Yuji and Otter divide the Ninjans into four teams of attack - their mission - to create as much confusion as possible with Smoke Bombs, Explosions, Whistle Arrows, and Physical Combat. Prior to attack, the leaders will sneak to the edge of Camp and hide. When the loud diversions begin - Yuji, Bear Claw, Otter, Two Knives and Eagle Feather, will sneak through the War Camp to Storm Cloud's tepee to capture him. All the Raiding Party agree to wait for Yuji's signal. As the sun drops low, and daylight lessens and shadows increase, Yuji and the leaders quietly sneak their way down the elevation point, across the wide Canyon floor to hide near the edge of Camp. Bear Claw and Yuji know exactly where to find the tepee with the War Lance imbedded in the ground out front. The sun dips lower and the high Canyon walls are soon covered with dark shadow. The time is ripe for attack. Yuji takes an arrow fitted with a narrow tube, draws back his bow and shoots the arrow high above the Camp. Yuji's arrows sends out a trail of bright red powder - the signal to attack. Mountain Bird and the Ninjans see Yuji's signal arrow and start their assault. The four Ninjan teams let loose explosion grenades, fire loud Whistle arrows, and lob smoke bombs into various sections of the wide Camp. The War Party braves are getting ready for the evening, to settle down, eat, and get some rest.

## SUDDENLY!    EXPLOSIONS EVERYWHERE!    THICK SMOKE BOMBS

The rogue braves are shocked, surprised and confused! Explosions happen across the Camp, and fires suddenly flare up putting tepees, tents, and shelters in danger. Both the horses and the braves are startled! Thick smoke fills the air and the braves have difficulty seeing. People are running everywhere in the confusion. Now, is the time for Yuji, Bear Claw, and the Ninjans to go capture Storm Cloud. The Shoshone quickly run to the target tepee, following Yuji as he leads them through the Camp and between various dwelling until they reach the tepee with the War Lance. Yuji and the others swiftly duck for cover because Storm Cloud stands outside his tepee with Grey Wolf and Running Elk. A few War Party braves stand nearby. All around the Camp - fires are raging, Storm Cloud hears explosions and sees dense smoke hanging in the air. The Chief turns to Grew Wolf and remarks, "Is it the White Man's Army soldiers?" Grey Bird shakes his head and replies, "I do not know great Chief!" As Storm Cloud is engaged and distracted - Yuji, Bear Claw, Otter, Two Knives, and Eagle Feather race to attack. The young Chief and those with him are surprised and caught off guard. The nearby rogue warriors try to protect their Chief, and Yuji and Otter unleash their Ninjan fighting skills to destroy and decimate them - their bodies lay in the dirt. Grey Wolf and Running Elk, both powerful warriors, step out to fight. With knife in one hand, and tomahawk in the other, Bear Claw confronts the younger Grey Wolf. Off to the side, Two Knives with a big blade in each hand, faces Running Elk in combat. The two sets of Indian warriors battle one another. Grey Wolf chooses to face Bear Claw the same way, with knife in one hand and tomahawk in the other. It appears both are equally matched. Grey Wolf swipes the knife blade, and swings the tomahawk at his opponent's head. Bear Claw swiftly ducks, blocks the knife swing, and twirls the tomahawk to knock the tomahawk out of Grey Wolf's hand. Now, the young brave uses his knife to lunge at Bear Claw. The older experienced warrior quickly steps to the side and hits Grey Wolf on the head, knocking him unconscious. Off the right, Running Elk and Two Knives are locked in fierce combat, wrestling with each other, attempting to toss the other to the ground. Running Elk is strong and the Shoshone Scout strains against his younger opponent. Running Elk holds his knife blade inches away from Two Knives' face - pushing and pressing the blade closer and closer. Two Knives' eyes are focused on the sharp blade inching toward his eyes. In the tense struggle, Two Knives senses weakness as Running Elk tries to regain strength - that is the moment Two Knives strikes. The Shoshone warrior sweeps his leg to knock his attacker off-balance, then the mature warrior throws the young brave hard to the ground. THUD! Two Knives immediately jumps on top his opponent and holds the sharp blade against the vulnerable skin of Running Elk's neck. Running Elk stops struggling and lays defeated. Two Knives grabs a rock on the ground and knocks out the feisty warrior. With turmoil and calamity all around, Storm Cloud takes a deep breath, straightens up, flexes his muscles, and stands ready to fight. The young Chief is visibly muscular and very strong -someone with the strength to kill another. The young Chief looks the intruders and taunts, "I will fight any one of you. It does not matter for I will win!" Filled with bravado and arrogance, Storm Cloud stands poised for combat. Bear Claw, Two Knives, Eagle Feather, Yuji and Otter observe the rogue Chief before them. Bear Claw glances about and realizes their time to escape grows small, he remarks, "Yuji. Let Storm Cloud learn of Ninjans!" Storm Cloud smirks and chides, "Ninjans. (Laughs) What is Ninjans?" Yuji steps out, assumes a Ninjan fighting stance, and replies, "I guarantee you - today you will find out!" The young Chief looks at Yuji in battle form with curiosity, and Storm Cloud launches out to attack. The strong young Chief swings his tomahawk and Yuji summersaults backward to land on his feet to face his opponent. Storm Cloud forcefully swipes his big knife blade again and again, Yuji bobs and weaves to avoid each attack. In a rage, Storm Cloud rushes forward, Yuji grabs the young man's arm and flips him hard to the ground. THUD! Storm Cloud is dazed and quickly springs to his feet. He repeatedly swings the tomahawk and swipes the blade in anger. Yuji blocks the tomahawk and knife attacks, then Yuji pummels Storm Cloud with crippling Martial Arts blows again and again - causing the muscular young warrior to crumple to the ground. Storm Cloud lifts his eyes just in time to see Yuji apply a chokehold that renders the rogue Chief unconscious. Bear Claw and Yuji quickly lift up Storm Cloud's body, and the Shoshone leaders carry an unconscious Storm Cloud, through the smoke and explosions, past War Party tepees, to reach their escape route. Quickly, the leaders join up with the Ninjans, Mountain Bird, and their horses. They securely tie Storm Cloud on the back of Bear Claw's horse, and the Raiding Party steal away. Within the chaos-filled Camp, War Party braves are at their wits-end, trying to put out fires, clear away smoke, calm their horses and hundreds of cattle, and are greatly puzzled why their Chief and leaders have disappeared.

# CHAPTER FIFTEEN

## *Return to Shoshone Lands*

Bear Claw, Yuji, and the Raiding Party, speed their way through the rock formations, and soon reach the open space of the grassy tundra. With the grasslands before them, the Shoshone Raiding Party ride hard toward their Tribal lands. The Shoshone warriors in the back, keep a lookout for any rogue braves that would be after them. No one follows. None of Storm Cloud's warriors are in pursuit. The Shoshone and the Ninjans race their horses across the massive Plains, through rolling grasslands, over brooks and streams, and up and down wilderness vales. Eventually, the group leave the open tundra to enter the fields and forests that are part of Shoshone Tribal territory. Taking familiar paths through the tall pines and leafy oaks, and traveling hunting trails through the thick brush, the Raiding Party come out to a wide open space where they behold their home. The Shoshone Camp sits snug on the gentle bend of a wide river, the river provides water for drinking, cooking, and cleansing. The Tribe's many tepees are spread out with comfortable space between each dwelling. Bear Claw, Eagle Feather, Two Knives, Yuji, Otter, and the other braves, smile at the sight of their Camp. Bear Claw sees smoke rising from the large central tepee. The seasoned leader knows that inside the structure, Chief Buffalo Sky and the Elders sit at a Council Fire. The Raiding Party move slowly toward Camp, many of them are tired from their difficult mission. Villagers at the edge of Camp see the returning warriors and sound out their arrival. Soon, many villagers stir at the news of the Raiding Party's return. People exit tepees to join others who walk alongside and behind the returning warriors. The noise of excitement and people's voices alert Chief Buffalo Sky and the Elders that something important is taking place. The Chief and Elders exit the big tepee and stand at the entrance. They watch as the Raiding Party draws near, then stops before them. The Shoshone villagers are filled with happiness that the Raiding Party has come home safe. Chief Buffalo Sky raises his arm in the air - the sign for all to be still. Immediately, the people stop talking, and all become quiet to pay attention. As the entire Shoshone village looks on, Chief Buffalo Sky takes a couple paces forward and remarks, "Welcome home my brothers! How was the Raid?" Bear Claw and the other leaders dismount and respectfully stand before their revered Chief. Bear Claw steps up before Buffalo Sky, then turns to the Raiding Party and motions with his hand. Chief Buffalo Sky and the Elders watch as three strong braves escort a tightly bound Indian warrior from the back of the group. With a Shoshone brave on each side, in addition to a brave behind, the captive is marched up to stand before them. Chief Buffalo Sky's eye brows raise, all the Elders are wide-eyed, for Storm Cloud stands before them with clenched teeth and a cold stare. Storm Cloud's countenance says it all - his face full of defiance - his eyes filled with anger and hatred! Chief Buffalo Sky carefully studies the rogue troublemaker, then calmly remarks, "We will take you before the Council of Chiefs!" Storm Cloud bursts out LAUGHING and shouts, "I am Storm Cloud! I honour no Council of Chiefs (spits on ground) Old men with old ways. (Lifts head proud) I bring the Indians new ways - My ways!" Buffalo Sky steps close to the rogue Chief and replies, "Your ways are the ways of death - Death for the Indians and the White Man!" Storm Cloud struggles against those holding him, as he tries to confront the Shoshone Chief, "The Paleface will leave our lands. Storm Cloud will make War!" The eyes of Chief Buffalo Sky sadden, and the Chief responds, "Peace is better than war! Indians and the White Man live together. Best for all!" Storm Cloud smirks and gives a rebuttal, "I am a new Chief. Strong and smart!" Chief Buffalo Sky points his finger at the young warrior and sternly rebukes, "You are nothing but a fool!" Having heard enough, and realizing the case with Storm Cloud is hopeless, Chief Buffalo Sky shakes his head, then signals to Bear Claw and the other leaders, "Take him away - his heart and mind are filled with poison! He is evil and dead inside!" As the Raiding Party braves forcibly takes Storm Cloud away, the rebellious Chief yells as he's being dragged away, "My warriors will rescue me! My warriors will rescue me!" The prisoner's words alarm the Shoshone villagers, and many become fearful, having heard the stories about Storm Cloud's vicious War Party. Chief Buffalo Sky sees the concern among his people, and he raises his arm and lifts his voice loud and clear, "My people - Do not Fear! The great Indian Chiefs will deal with Storm Cloud! The War Party will be no more!" The assurance from their Chief calms the Shoshone villagers, and the people go back to their daily chores and activities. As the villagers disperse, Chief Buffalo Sky motions to the tepee entrance, and comments, "Join the Council Fire. Tell us of the Raid." At the Chief's invitation, Bear Claw, Yuji, Two Knives, Eagle Feather, and Otter, step into the large central tepee. After Otter has stepped through the opening, he reaches to pull down the entrance cover.

The Shoshone warriors guarding Storm Cloud cart him to a designated tepee set aside to hold the rogue Chief. The braves bring in their prisoner and bind his arms behind his back. Next, the braves insert a thick hardwood pole between Storm Cloud's arms and his back. Then, the braves tie the young Chief's arms to the pole with strong leather cords. Storm Cloud attempts to struggle, but he's bound tight and secure, unable to use his arms or hands. The Shoshone guards force the rogue leader to sit on the ground, where the braves bind Storm Cloud's feet. Unable to use his limbs, and unable to move his legs, Storm Cloud sits on the tepee floor posing no threat. Bear Claw gave orders that two guards must always be inside watching the prisoner, and two braves outside the entrance to guard the tepee. As the two Shoshone braves keep their eyes on him, Storm Cloud looks at his captors with a scowl of disgust.

# CHAPTER SIXTEEN

## *The Council of Chiefs*

Chief Buffalo Sky sends riders to the different Indian Tribes to inform the Chiefs that Storm Cloud is captured, and being held in the Shoshone Camp. The Chiefs send back word that they will be at the Council of Chiefs, set for the next new moon in three weeks. There is ample time for each Tribal Chief to make the journey to attend the important gathering. Over the years, the Council of Chiefs has only met a couple of times to deal with matters that affected all the Indian Tribes. The last occasion was the signing of the Peace Treaty sent from the White Man's Great Chief in Washington. The destruction and death caused by Storm Cloud has deeply troubled the Tribal Chiefs. Now, the brash rogue warrior must stand before all the Plains' Chiefs, and face their punishment.

Over the next two weeks, Bear Claw and Eagle Feather ensure that Storm Cloud is fed and well cared for. The two leaders take extra steps to keep their captive protected by doubling their efforts - putting four braves inside, and four warriors outside the guard the tepee. Yuji has Ninjans hidden throughout Shoshone lands, to act as sentries to warn of any intruders or attacks. Chief Buffalo Sky, the Elders, and the lead warriors are satisfied that all is well - their captive, their village, and their important Council - are all set and secure!

Hosting the Council of Chiefs is a great honour among the Indian Tribes. The last Meeting was held by the Sioux Nation for the signing the White Man's Peace Treaty. With three weeks before the Chiefs arrive, Buffalo Sky has time to construct the Great Tepee where the Tribal Chiefs will meet. The Great Tepee must house all the Chiefs and their important lead warriors. Average tepees of the Plains Indians are 20 and sometimes 30 feet tall. Chief Buffalo Sky gives orders for braves to go to the forest and cut down trees three times the regular length and bring them back to Camp. The Shoshone braves led by Eagle Feather, Two Knives, and Bear Claw, find trees that soar 100 feet high in the forest. With painstaking effort, the Shoshone braves chop down the towering wood giants, and use teams of horses to drag the tall timber back to Camp. Adjacent to the Shoshone Village itself, an enormous clearing has been selected to erect the Great Tepee. The construction starts by lashing three timbers together at the top with thick braided leather cords and heavy rope. Teams of horses and scores of manpower strain to pull the tall timbers upright to form a tripod. When the three towering poles are anchored into the ground, teams of Shoshone workers pull the other support poles into place. Shoshone braves unafraid of heights, work at the very top, fitting and lashing each timber secure to the others, thus creating the soaring framework for the Great Tepee. Shoshone women and young maidens prepare, cut, and sew canvass to create large sheets which will be used to cover the structure. The men use teams of horses to draw the fabric around the support poles, then attach the fabric as a tepee cover. Shoshone people gifted with artistic talent mix wild berries, flowers, plants, trees leaves, and bark, to create coloured pigment. The artists paint the exterior of the Great Tepee with Shoshone Tribal art and decorations. When it's all completed, Chief Buffalo Sky, the Elders, Bear Claw, Yuji, and the lead warriors, stand spell-bound before the giant structure that soars high above the ground. The Great Tepee will have enough room for all the Chiefs and their entourage to sit for the important Council. Chief Buffalo Sky instructs braves to pile wood at a safe distance away for the giant bonfire, that will be lit commence the beginning the Council of Chiefs. The entire Village is excited that so many of the Plains Indian Chiefs will be their Camp. All the Shoshone are filled with Tribal pride.

The day of the new moon, Indian Chiefs from the different Tribes arrive with Tribal Elders and delegates. Chief Buffalo Sky wears his tan buckskin tunic and leggings that features ornate bead patterns, leather frills, and shiny silver disks. The old leader looks proud and noble in his Shoshone Chief's Bonnet of eagle feathers, decorative beadwork, and small coloured poms. Buffalo Sky stands regal and stately beside the Elders, as he officially welcomes the arrival of the other Chiefs.

Shoshone warriors dressed in their best attire are assembled and stand nearby. Everyone is thrilled and excited to see so many leaders of the Plains' Indian Tribes in their Camp. Buffalo Sky and the Elders are pleased to see the neighbouring tribes - the **Crow**, **Blackfoot**, **Arapaho**, **Flathead**, and **Cheyenne**. The Shoshone Chief, Elders, and Warriors, are delighted to see the various Chiefs and warriors from Tribes far away - the **Sioux**, **Pawnee**, **Dakota**, and **Kiowa**. The scene is stunning with the various Chiefs in their spectacular Bonnets and Tribal attire. The assembled Indian warriors from across the Great Plains is once-in-a-lifetime experience, everyone in attendance feels the significance of this historic moment. Each Chief sits atop his horse surrounded by his Tribe's warriors. When all have arrived in Camp, there is a quiet respectful lull, the only noise heard is the wind in the trees, and the pawing of hooves on the ground, and the intermittent whine of horses. Everyone is quiet and silent. Gazing out at his assembled guests, Chief Buffalo Sky steps out to raise his arms as he looks about, and declares, "Welcome mighty Chiefs and important warriors! The Shoshone people are greatly honoured at your presence in our Camp! Let the Council of Chiefs begin in the Great Tepee - where we can rest, eat, and talk at our Great Council!" At Buffalo Sky's words and invitation, the Indian Chiefs and their entourage dismount and make their way into the towering structure, where there is food, drink, and blankets to sit upon. Chief Buffalo Sky stands beside the big entrance to greet and welcome each of his fellow Chiefs. Once all the Tribal leaders and warriors have entered inside, Buffalo Sky signals to the braves standing next to the giant wood pile. Immediately, the braves take burning sticks out of small fires, and throw the fire brands high up on the massive pile of wood. Soon, the Bonfire begins to burn bright to announce the official start of the Great Council of Chiefs. As flames shoot up from the Bonfire, the ceremony from inside the Great Tepee fills the outside air with the sounds of pounding drums, and hundreds of warriors loudly chanting!

Inside the Great Tepee's massive interior, all the Indian Chiefs position to form a large Great Council circle. Sitting crosslegged on the ground behind each Chief, are that Tribe's Elders and delegated warriors. Stationed behind Chief Buffalo Sky are the Shoshone Elders, and Bear Claw, Eagle Feather, Two Knives, Yuji, and Otter. While the big interior reverberates with the pounding drums and loud chants, Chief Buffalo Sky raises his arm - and all becomes quiet. The wise old leader gazes at the faces of the Indian Chiefs before him, and he remarks, "Storm Cloud's wild actions have hurt Indian Tribes and the White Man. (The Chiefs nod) We will bring this renegade warrior before the Council of Chiefs. It is for the Chiefs to decide what must be done!" Chief Buffalo Sky waves his hand to signal that Storm Cloud be brought before the Great Council. From the far back of the wide interior, four big Shoshone warriors bring forth Storm Cloud with hands tied, escorting the rogue warrior to stand in front of all the Great Council. All the Chiefs fix their eyes on the young warrior, for many, it is the first time they see the troublesome culprit. The rogue leader stands straight and lifts his chin in a proud manner. Storm Cloud boldly stares back at the assembled Chiefs, the scene is that of a young brave facing a group of older Indian Warriors. Storm Cloud takes deep breaths that makes his big chest heave. He e adjusts his body position, and the muscles in legs and his strong arms flex. There is no doubt about it - Storm Cloud is a prime specimen of a strong young Indian warrior. Nevertheless, Storm Cloud's greedy ambition for power, his open disregard of Tribal leaders, and his bloody attacks on the White Man - is the very reason the Council of Chiefs must decide his fate.

The great leader of the **Sioux**, "**Chief Jumping Horse**", points at the young instigator and declares, "You have damaged our Peace Treaty with the White Man! (Pause) You have taken young braves from our Tribes to be your warriors - speaking to them with a forked tongue!" The other Chiefs nod in agreement. Storm Cloud smirks as he replies, "The Peace Treaty takes away our Freedom. Your braves flock to me because I will make Indians great once more." The various Elders and warriors sitting around, carefully watch and listen to the exchange of words. "**Chief Spotted Owl**" of the **Blackfoot** reprimands the arrogant leader, "You give Whiskey to our people! The Fire Water clouds the mind and heart! It brings trouble to our lands!" Storm Cloud gives a surly reply, "White Men drink the Fire Water - Indians must drink also! Fire Water gives courage for battle!" Murmur and chatter ripples through the Great Tepee at the wild leader's remark. The respected leader of the **Crow**, "**Chief Little Hawk**", rebukes the young brave, "You have spilled the blood of White Men - and the blood of Indians." Storm Cloud braces with defiance and gives a rebuttal, "War brings death - But War will chase away the Intruders from our lands. War will make the Indian Tribes mighty again!" Some of the Chiefs hang their heads, sad to hear such venom from such a promising young warrior.

The aged leader of the **Arapaho**, "**Chief Fighting Bear**", lifts his hand toward the young man and remarks, "The Indian Tribes are mighty! Our Tribal language, customs, and ways, give us a special pride!" Seated beside him, the Tribal leader of the **Kiowa**, "**Chief Leaping Wolf**" chides, "Do you place yourself above the great Council of Chiefs?" Storm Cloud LAUGHS to everyone's horror, and the brash young warrior replies with a clear arrogant tone, "You are old men with old ways! Something from the past.(Smirk) Storm Cloud is a new Chief - with new ways for Indian braves!" At this moment, Chief Buffalo Sky cries out, "Your ways are the ways of stealing - killing - and death - Death for the White Man and Indians!" The heated exchange between Storm Cloud and the Chiefs has reached a peak, and the entire Tepee is abuzz with comment and intense conversation, all the attendees responding to what they've heard. Storm Cloud looks around the cavernous interior and delights in the fact he is the cause of all this commotion. The rogue leader revels at all the attention. As the conversations of Indian braves, Elders, and Chiefs rises to become louder and louder - Chief Buffalo Sky stands to his feet and raises his arms high. Conversations cease across the tepee interior. The Shoshone Chief looks at his fellow Chiefs and remarks, "We have heard from his own mouth - and looked into his own heart. Now, it is time, we must decide the fate of Storm Cloud!" Buffalo Sky sits down and watches as the Council of Chiefs quietly confer together. When the Chiefs stop talking, the revered leader of the **Cheyenne, "Chief Burning Arrow"**, stands to his feet, approaches Storm Cloud, and remarks, "The Council of Chiefs have decided your fate - Because you have stole, destroyed, and killed the Paleface - we turn you over to the White Man. He will judge you for the evil done. The White Man will imprison you in a great stone house - or he take away your life.(pause, scans room) No matter what, your fate is in their hands!" Storm Cloud watches as all the Indian Chiefs nod their heads in solidarity. The Council of Chiefs' decision has been made, the judgement set - the wild rebellious rogue Chief, Storm Cloud, will face the White Man's punishment!

The enormous Bonfire burns bright illuminating the Giant Tepee on the night of the Council of Chiefs. The sound of many pounding drums and loud chanting fills the evening air, as hundreds of warriors from the different Tribes join together to stomp and dance in celebration. The Tribal Chiefs stand together to watch the closing festivities of the Great Council. The scene is a spectacle to behold - to witness the various Indian warriors dressed in their tribal attire, circling the giant bonfire in united solidarity. - This was indeed a glorious moment, the Tribes of the Great Plains working together for the good of all Indians! Chief Buffalo Sky and his fellow Chieftains smile with pride at their collective warriors performing the closing ritual, the "Dance of Many Tribes". The Indian braves fill the air with jubilant YELLS, CELEBRATION CRIES, and VICTORY SHOUTS!

With the sunrise of a new day, Chief Buffalo Sky, the Elders, and the lead warriors, bid farewell as the different Chiefs and their entourages depart. The Shoshone villagers watch their guests with interest as they ride their horses out of camp. Many of the Shoshone people will never again get a glimpse of the different Tribes that journeyed to their village. For the Shoshone people, the Council of Chiefs will be remembered in their legend and lore. One of the last groups to leave are the Blackfoot. It was the decision of the Chiefs that Storm Cloud would be taken to Army soldiers at the White Man's fort near the lands of the Blackfoot. Their leader, "Chief Spotted Owl" agreed to transport the rogue warrior to the Fort. Chief Spotted Owl sits atop his stallion, near him is Storm Cloud securely bound on horseback, surrounded by many Blackfoot warriors. Spotted Owl gives a parting wave to Chief Buffalo Sky and the Elders, and the Blackfoot delegation ride off heading out of Camp.

# CHAPTER SEVENTEEN

## *Rogue Warriors Attack*

Chief Spotted Owl and the Blackfoot group ride through the tall grass that covers the rolling terrain of the Great Plains. Storm Cloud rides hemmed in with Blackfoot braves in front, behind, and on both sides of him. The reins of the rogue warrior's horse is held and led by the Blackfoot braves in front. The sky is clear without a cloud in sight, and the temperature is warm. Only a slight breeze blows across the landscape. In the distance ahead, the rolling grassland gives way to forest growth, the wilderness trees dense and thick with foliage. As the Blackfoot group approach the woods - Suddenly,  Grey Wolf and hundreds of War Party braves ride out the trees with SCREAMS, YELLS, and WAR CRIES! Chief Spotted Owl and group bolt their horses to the right to avoid the oncoming attackers. The small group begin to put distance between them and the pursuing warriors. As the Blackfoot braves scan ahead to seek an escape route, to their shock, Running Elk and hundreds of additional War Party braves rush out from a deep vale that hid them. Caught in the middle, Chief Spotted Owl and his warriors get ready to fight their way through. By now, the small Blackfoot group is encircled, totally surrounded by hostile War Party braves. Everyone stops - the two groups stare at each other. Then, Grey Wolf motions his arm. Hundreds of braves fire their rifles up into the air. A sounds of gunshots ring out in the air and envelope the Blackfoot entourage. Grey Wolf and two braves ride out to stop in front of the Blackfoot Chief. Grey Wolf remarks to the older warrior, "Release our Chief Storm Cloud, and we will let you and your warriors live!" Chief Spotted Owl looks out at the hundreds of fierce armed War Party braves - he gazes upon his warriors; then, he looks at Storm Cloud who sits with an arrogant smirk. The Blackfoot Chief knows there is no chance against such odds - it would be a senseless slaughter. Chief Spotted Owl directs his eyes to one of his lead warriors and orders, "Untie Storm Cloud!" The warrior and braves around their captive untie and loosen the bonds holding the rogue leader. Storm Cloud pulls apart the cords which fall to the ground. He grabs the reins, looks at Chief Spotted Owl and comments, "You chose well old man! You and your warriors will live (grins) and tell other Indians how Storm Cloud is mighty - and can never be bound!" The young Chief kicks his horse and bolts forward to join Grey Wolf. When he reaches alongside his warrior friend, Storm Cloud lifts his arm high, waves and rides out. Immediately, the War Party respond to follow their leader. Chief Spotted Owl and his braves watch in silence as Storm Cloud and his massive force ride away. A Blackfoot brave asks the Chief, "What of the Council of Chiefs?" The old Blackfoot Chief replies, "Storm Cloud lives (puts hand on brave's shoulder) And we live also!" Chief Spotted Owl signals with his hand, and the Blackfoot warriors move in the direction of their Tribal lands, toward familiar tepees and their families.

Chief Spotted Owl and the Blackfoot warriors finally reach home, and are happy to see their loved ones, and are deeply grateful their lives were spared. The next day, riders are dispatched near and far, to tell the Chiefs that Storm Cloud has escaped. The terrible news sends dread through the various tribes, making them fear what the rebellious young Chief will do next. News reaches back to the Shoshone Camp and brings alarm to Buffalo Sky, the Elders, and the lead warriors. Bear Claw, Eagle Feather, Yuji and Otter can only imagine the reign of terror that Storm Cloud will unleash across the Plains. Something must be done - but what? No Tribe has the warriors, nor the will, to go up against the rogue Chief and his horde of crazed braves.

# CHAPTER EIGHTEEN

*Fires Across The Plains*

Released from his captivity, Storm Cloud is emboldened with an increased desire to see the havoc, destruction, and death of his enemies. With a renewed sense of his twisted purpose, Storm Cloud and his hundreds of War Party braves attack locomotive trains, killing passengers, pillaging supplies, and setting railroad cars on fire. The blood-curdling SCREAMS and WAR CRIES bring shock and fear, as Storm Cloud and his fierce warriors attack Mining Camps, Stagecoach Stations, Farms, Ranches, and Homesteads. All across the Plains, fires burn and smoke billows as signs of raids by the War Party. Peoples' hearts are griped with fear at the mention of the name - Storm Cloud!

Ranch houses, Cattle Barns, Livery Stables, Stagecoaches, Telegraph Offices, and family homes, are burned to the ground; their blacken ashes a dreadful sign that Storm Cloud struck there. Impending Indian attacks have Settlers, Townsfolk, Ranchers, and Politicians living in fear. Everyone is fully aware of the brutality of Storm Cloud's vicious drunken braves. Indian warriors liquored up on Whiskey, and poisoned by the rogue Chief's venomous rants against his enemies. People, no matter their background; Irish, Polish, German, Ukrainian; and no matter their skin colour; Black, White, Chinese, or Spanish; everyone is worried for their life! Communities post local volunteers to act as sentries to lookout for marauding bands of War Party braves. Companies hire extra armed guards to ride escort for traveling Stagecoaches. Ranchers make Cowboys ride in groups because safety is in numbers. Even the different Indian Tribes are on edge because Storm Cloud wants to cause a War with the White Man. The Indian Chiefs want to avoid this at all cost!

* * *

The sleepy town of SMOOTH ROCK with its Stagecoach Stop, is situated in close proximity to Indian lands. It wasn't too long ago that the community had lots residents. But many people have left from fear of Indian attacks. Now, the locals are down to a handful of citizens. The tiny hamlet has a dry goods Mercantile, Blacksmith Shop, Livery Stable, Barbershop, and a Saloon. With most folks gone, local merchants have few customers. In the past, the streets were filled with people visiting town, buying supplies, or wetting appetites at the Saloon. Now, the only sign of life on town streets are rolling tumble weeds, stray dogs, and the odd old timer. It seems even amid Indian attacks all across the Plains, everyone has forgotten about Smooth Rock. However, that's about to change. Out in the wilderness terrain, Storm Cloud, Grey Wolf and Running Elk, watch the town as they're sitting on their horses. Storm Cloud grins and snaps an order, "Attack the little White Man's village! Burn everything!" Grey Wolf responds by waving his arm in the air to signal four hundred War Party braves to attack. The residents are going about their daily affairs when SCREAMS, YELLS, and WAR CRIES pierce the air. Some men look out on the horizon to see the terrible sight of hundreds of Indian warriors riding hard toward town. The townsmen sound out the alarm, and everyone runs to hide behind closed doors. In minutes, War Party braves stream into town from all directions, riding through the streets, YELLING and SCREAMING. The Warriors fire their rifles to break glass windows, shoot fire arrows at wood structures, and toss burning torches inside buildings. The men and women of the town defend themselves, and shoot their guns at the attacking braves, wounding and killing many. By now, every wood structure is ablaze, with roofs, walls, and doors, on fire. Thick black smoke creeps indoors making the people cough and struggle to breath. In desperation, many attempt to flee the flames by escaping outside, others remain inside and resign themselves to a fiery death. The Townsfolk who left burning buildings to escape the flames, are met with bullets and arrows from fierce warriors. Men, women, and children, are slaughtered by War Party braves. The dead lay in doorways, on boardwalks, and in the dusty street, their bodies full of arrows and bullet holes. The crackling sound of burning wood fills the air, and dark smoke fills the sky. At Grey Wolf's signal, the rogue braves ride out of the destroyed hamlet. Storm Cloud has a sinister smile as he observes the death and destruction left by his War Party. With the residents of Smooth Rock dead and the buildings burning to the ground, Storm Cloud and his rogue warriors ride away.

Back at their Camp, Storm Cloud arranges scores of Whiskey barrels to supply his warriors with liquor. The young men drink the booze with abandon, even pouring it over each other's heads like some kind of warrior ritual. The young braves drink themselves into a stupor, many falling down unable to walk, others are passed out, and a large number vomit from drinking too much. The scene is organized chaos as different groups of braves, YELL and SCREAM at the top of their lungs, and shoot rifles in the air. All across the sprawling Camp, braves lay on the ground passed out, others are hunched over vomiting, and here and there fights break out. As he looks out over the Camp, Storm Cloud doesn't mind allowing his warriors to let off steam and exhibit their wildness. He knows that if he can keep them plied with liquor and focused on a common enemy - his horde of wild braves will eventually rid the entire territory of all Paleface. Storm Cloud gloats as he continues to watch his drunken warriors.

# CHAPTER NINETEEN
### *Trouble At Dry Gulch*

Chief Buffalo Sky, the Elders, and the Shoshone warriors, gather in the central tepee for a Council Fire. The men realize the gathering is important and wait in anticipation for their Chief to speak. Everyone patiently wait as they quietly talk, and periodically watch the dancing flames of the Council Fire. Chief Buffalo Sky lifts up his hand and all conversations stops. Buffalo Sky looks at his leaders and warriors, and remarks, "Bear Claw and Yuji have important information to tell us." The Chief extends his hand to the two Tribal leaders. Bear Claw lifts his voice for all to hear, "Storm Cloud gives his young warriors Whiskey! (Pause) We know how the renegade Chief gets the Whiskey!" The tepee interior ripples with comment and chatter at the information shared. The Shoshone warriors rivet their attention on Bear Claw as he continues, "White Traders sell Whiskey to Storm Cloud. The Traders live at a place in the wilds called Dry Gulch!" Again, the tepee is filled with noise as the braves talk back and forth. Chief Buffalo Sky raises his hand and all the warriors become quiet. Bear Claw remarks, "Two Knives will lead us to the Traders' Camp. Yuji, Otter, and our Ninjans, will destroy their Whiskey supply!" The Shoshone Elders and the warriors nod in agreement at hearing the plan. Chief Buffalo Sky stands up, looks out at his warriors and declares, "Bear Claw, Eagle Feather, Two Knives, Yuji, and Otter, will stop Storm Cloud getting Whiskey!" The entire assembly stand to their feet, and with loud voice let out SHOUTS of Victory!

Early next morning, Chief Buffalo Sky and the Elders, stand outside the central tepee. The Tribal leaders look at their Shoshones warriors on horseback before them. Buffalo Sky lifts his hand high and declares,

"Ride Swift. Be Strong. Fight Well. Return Victorious!" With the CHief's words still in their ear, the Shoshone braves ride out of Camp toward the forests and hills, heading to the expansive wilds, where the ground is dry and plants are few. The Wilds is a desolate place, home to rattlesnakes, scorpions, coyotes, and vultures. Settlers, farmers, and ranchers, reject the place knowing that there's nothing of value there. The fact others avoid this inhospitable terrain is exactly why the Traders made their Camp in such wretched ground. The Traders are free to operate their sketchy enterprise without any interference or prying eyes. That is what makes it a haven for the shady characters that call Dry Gulch home. It a den of iniquity, an assortment of cons, swindlers, sly merchants, and unscrupulous traders.

Two Knives leads the Shoshone warriors through Tribal lands, over grasslands, across rocky terrain, until they reach the Wilds. The braves tag behind their veteran Scout, as he guides the warrior group across unfamiliar ground. Two Knives follows the horse tracks left behind by men that made their way to the Traders' wilderness Hideout. None of the Shoshone have ever been in this environment before, this trek into the Wilds is totally new territory, many braves wonder what lays ahead. Two Knives peers down at the hoof prints in the parched ground, then lifts his head to look to the horizon, and the ridge on the left. He turns to Bear Claw, points and remarks, "I will go alone to the ridge. Keep the others here." Bear Claw nods. The Shoshone Scout dismounts and moves toward the ridge. As he gets near, Two Knives crawls to the ridge and carefully peers over the crest. In a few moments, Two Knives returns and comments, "The Traders' Camp is below the ridge - hidden from view." Bear Claw looks at Yuji and remarks, "The Traders are below the ridge. You and Otter spy out the Camp. Tell us what is there." Yuji and Otter nod. The two Ninjan Masters dismount and quickly move to the crest of the ridge. Yuji and Otter scan their eyes at the Traders' Camp stretched out in front of them. It's a ramshackle cluster of wood buildings, canvass tents, tin sheds, and adobe shelters, joined together in a rough haphazard way. As the two Ninjans continue to spy out the encampment, the Shoshone braves tend to the horses to make sure the animals stay quiet. The Shoshone watch as the two Ninjans, suddenly disappear over the ridge out of sight.

Yuji and Otter sneak down the slope and conceal themselves behind wood crates and empty barrels piled at the side of a wood shed. The buildings have walls, tarp barriers, and wood fences, that zigzag back and forth, providing lots nooks and dark spaces to hide and spy from. Some men in the Trader encampment move about going in and out of tents and huts. As Yuji and Otter ease their way along the exterior walls, they hear the conversations going on inside. Yuji stops and peeks through a crack between the bleached boards of a shelter - he sees men sitting at a table playing cards, and drinking liquor from dusty bottles. On the other side of the interior, individuals are stretched out on cots, a few are asleep. Yuji taps Otter and gives a forward motion. Both warriors are dressed in their Ninjan black outfit, armed with their Ninjato and Katana swords, sharp Shuriken stars, Ninjan Tomahawk, knives, and black leather pouches with explosive bombs. The residents of Dry Gulch move about their business, unaware of the two Ninjans hidden in the shadows. Yuji and Otter secretly move from structure to structure, noticing the inhabitants are - old Muleskinners, thick bearded Miners, mean-looking Cowboys, fancy-dressed businessmen, rugged workers, and raggedy Traders. Traveling throughout the Trader settlement, Yuji and Otter do not see any barrels or supply of Whiskey. Then, Yuji signals Otter - a Trader pulls across a tarp cover that reveals the entrance to a tunnel that leads underground. After the man has entered the dark interior with his hand held torch, Yuji and Otter sneak behind to follow. The two Ninjans stay their distance as they tail the man walking further into the earthen tunnel. The man stops in a large opening that has four tunnel entrances. Yuji and Otter observe as the man enters the tunnel on the far left. Both Ninjans keep with their quarry in sight. Then, the moving torch stops. The man lights a torch embedded in the hard mud wall which illuminates the interior. To their surprise, Yuji and Otter see long rows of Whiskey barrels that fill the interior. Years ago, Prospectors used their mining skills to dig a complex of underground tunnels to store the Whiskey in a cool safe place. Yuji taps Otter to announce their departure. The Ninjan Masters retrace their way out the tunnel complex, through the Trader encampment, up the slope and back over the ridge. They rejoin Bear Claw and the warriors.

The seasoned leader and friend asks, "What did you find?" Yuji and Otter gaze upon Bear Claw and the others, and Yuji replies, "The Whiskey is stored in tunnels underneath the buildings!" Otter interjects, "Explosions will destroy the Whiskey supply!" Bear Claw and Eagle Feather smile at the Ninjan Leader's remark. Bear Claw turns to Yuji and comments, "Sketch out the Camp to help our attack." Yuji nods and begins to use a stick to draw the Camp layout in the sand. When complete, Yuji points to the building that has the tunnel entrance. And remarks, "We found tunnels below that lead to many Whiskey barrels." Bear Claw looks at his friend and questions, "Can the Ninjans put bombs to blow up the Whiskey?" Yuji and Otter nod with smiles. Bear Claw and Eagle Feather study the layout for a couple moments. Eagle Feather points to a section of the buildings, and comments, "If we attacked this spot - we will keep their guns and fighters busy - allowing Yuji, Otter and some Ninjans, to blow up the Whiskey supply!" Bear Claw is in quiet thought, then turns to Eagle Feather with a grin, "This is a good plan, old friend!" Yuji comments, "The attack will distract them - We will have great freedom to place our bombs." Everyone nods in approval at the attack plan. Bear Claw looks at the group of braves and instructs, "We break into two groups. Eagle Feather, myself and our Ninjans will attack the Camp at one end. Yuji, Otter and some others will blow up the Whiskey stored underground." All the braves nod acknowledgement. Bear Claw looks at Yuji, smiles and remarks, "Good Hunting my brother!" Yuji gives a hearty reply, "Fight well great warrior!" At this point, the group divides into two attack forces - one prepared to launch a strike at the far end of Camp - the other, Yuji, Otter and some Ninjans, ready to blow up the whiskey in the tunnels underground.

Yuji, Otter and several Ninjans, scurry to the crest of the ridge overlooking the Trader Camp, and wait for a signal. Bear Claw, Eagle Feather, Two Knives, and the rest of the Ninjans, move to the far end of wood structures, then spread out to take Attack positions. Both groups are poised for action - Two Knives gives a BIRD CALL as the signal to start. The Shoshone braves at the end of Camp let out loud SCREAMS, YELLS and WAR CRIES! They fire their rifles and shoot arrows at the buildings. The men inside raise the alarm - "Indians! Indians!" - and pour outside with guns ready. Other men from across the Camp rally to help their friends fight off the attack. The wood structures are peppered with arrows. The White Men see Bear Claw and the others, and begin to fire their Winchesters, shotguns, and pistols. Bear Claw and the braves duck for cover as a barrage of bullets hit the ground around them. The Shoshone fire back with their arrows and rifles - keeping the men of the encampment busy. Yuji, Otter and their Ninjans slip down to the shelters, and Yuji heads directly to the building with the tunnel entrance beneath it. As they enter the structure, they surprise two White Men who are guarding the entrance. Yuji and Otter quickly overpower and knock the men out. Otter pulls back the tarp cover to expose the tunnel entrance. The Ninjans light the nearby torches, and Yuji motions to follow. He leads them through the passageway and into the tunnel on the far left. As the Ninjans move deeper, light from their torches reveal Whiskey barrels stacked row upon row. With their Ninjan companions keeping guard, Yuji and Otter remove the bombs from their leather pouches, and place the explosives at key locations along the rows of barrels. When finished, Yuji and Otter rejoin the others in the large chamber. Yuji places his two remaining bombs with the barrels at the front. He lowers the flame of a lit torch to ignite the long fuse of the bomb - it sparks and begins to burn. The Ninjans immediately make a mad dash! They race out of the Whiskey chamber that's about to explode, through the tunnels, swiftly exit the wood structure, and run up and over the top of the ridge - and wait.

**EXPLOSIONS! TREMORS! FIREBALLS!**

The Trader encampment of Dry Gulch is blown apart! EXPLOSIONS and BLASTS ripe through the sheds, tents, and buildings. Fire and smoke is everywhere. The Ninjan bombs ignited the alcohol in the stored Whiskey barrels, producing powerful explosions that blew upward and outward, destroying buildings, levelling structures, and setting the place on fire. Dry Gulch, the haven of greedy Traders, has been turned into shattered buildings, burning rubble, deep craters, and scattered debris. The men who lived there were either killed, wounded, or run off. The entire settlement smoulders and lays in ruins. The two Indian groups meet up at the crest of the ridge and gaze below at the destruction. Bear Claw turns to Yuji, and comments, "This bad place is no more!" Yuji adds, "Storm Cloud's Whiskey is destroyed!" The Shoshone smile in victory as they watch the last remnants of the buildings catch fire and burn. Eagle Feather makes a remark that everyone's thinking, "Let us return home to our families and tepees." Everyone nods. The Shoshone warriors mount up on horseback, leave the demolished den of iniquity, and ride toward their Village and loved ones.

* * *

The next afternoon, a mule team pulling a wagon, arrives at the demolished site that was once Dry Gulch. Badger and Grit are shocked at the devastation of their former encampment. Nothing now, but scorched earth covered with ash and pieces of charred wood. The Traders cannot comprehend what happened! The two jump down off the wagon and start to walk through the burnt debris of former buildings, shelters, and tents. Checking through the rubble, Badger and Grit come across dead corpses, the bodies burned beyond any identification. They go to the location of the building that led to the underground tunnels - the men are stunned to see deep craters and sunken earth from cave-ins. Grit looks at his partner and asks, "What happened? Everything is gone!" Badger scans the area around and remarks, "These craters are from explosions! (Shakes head) Appears somehow the Whiskey blew up! That explains the burnt buildings and cave-ins." Grit comments, "What are we gonna do?" We got no more Whiskey!" Badger stretches tall, repositions his wide brim hat, and replies, "Find a place to start over!" The lean man has a fearful look, and utters, "What about Storm Cloud? With no more Whiskey - he'll be after us!" Badger quips, "That's why we gotta leave these parts real quick! (Serious tone) We can't trade anything if we're dead!" The two men make their way back to the wagon and climb up. Badger grabs the long whip and snaps it. CRACK! CRACK! The animals jolt alive and begin to pull. The Traders turns the wagon around, and leaves the soot and ash of Dry Gulch behind. Badger snaps the whip at the mule team. CRACK! The animals speed up, moving the wagon swiftly away from where they once stored their liquor. With no more Whiskey for his rogue warriors - Storm Cloud will turn against Badger and Grit - seeking their death!

# CHAPTER TWENTY

## *Storm Cloud's Wrath*

The sun in the Wilds is high above, blazing down on the parched dusty ground. At the crest of the ridge, five Indian warriors sit on horseback, as they stare at the burnt ruins of the Trader's former settlement. Grey Wolf motions his hand and the braves ride down the slope. They approach piles of blackened boards, all that's left of the buildings, and see the twisted metal tent poles contorted by the intense fire. Grey Wolf scans his eyes around at the site littered with soot, ash and charred debris. The brave moves his horse toward the location where he knows the Whiskey was stored - he looks at the craters and stretches of sunken earth, the result of cave-ins. Grey Wolf takes one last look around, then motions the group to leave. As the brave leads in front, his hunting skills alert him to the fresh wagon tracks on the ground. The warrior leader recognizes these wheel tracks - he has seen them before. A wagon wheel on the right side has a noticeable wobble that leaves a telltale sign. Grey Wolf knows these wagon tracks belong to Badger and Grit. The warrior quickens his horse to a fast gallop and races away, and the other braves swiftly follow him.

The War Camp is quiet and still - most of the young braves are tired, passed out, or sleeping it off after a wild night of partying. In the Chief's tepee, Running Elk and Storm Cloud are engaged in conversation when Grey Wolf announces from outside the dwelling, "We have returned!" Immediately, Storm Cloud and Running Elk exit the tepee to see their fellow warrior. Storm Cloud notices the sullen expression on his friend's face and remarks, "Your face is sour. What is wrong?" Grey Wolf glances at Running Elk, then looks at his Chief and replies, "The Trader Camp is totally burnt! Nothing remains!" The young Chief's eyes widen and he becomes angry, "What of the Whiskey? - My supply of Whiskey?" Grey Wolf responds, "No more Whiskey! Everything was destroyed! (Pause) The two Traders live - I saw fresh wagon tracks!" Storm Cloud is filled with rage as he grips the handle of his hunting knife, and yells, "Find the two Traders - Kill them! They promised many barrels of whiskey! (Scans Camp) Our braves need Whiskey!" Running Elk and Grey Wolf acknowledge their Chief's order with a nod. Both warriors quickly leave to assemble braves for a large Hunting Party - a Hunting Party to track down and kill - Badger and Grit.

Somewhere in the wilderness, the old muleskinner snaps the leather reins to make the mules go faster, the wheels of the wagon racing over the cracked dry ground. Every now and then, they glance over their shoulder, and take a quick glimpse at the horizon. The men certainly don't want to be found out in the open by any of Storm Cloud's War Party. The Traders know that it won't be long before the wild Chief gets news that there's no more Whiskey. Badger and Grit were foolish to promise Storm Cloud that he'd have a steady supply of the amber liquor. It was so important that Storm Cloud factored in the supply as a way to keep his warriors happy and motivated. With Whiskey unavailable - the hundreds of rowdy young warriors will become agitated, longing for the taste and the intoxicating effects of the booze. The rogue Chief must now devise a strategy to keep his braves busy and distracted. Nothing appeals to the bravado of young Indian braves that the challenge and excitement of a fight, and Storm Cloud plans to have many battles with the White Man. The young Chief knows that in the middle of a fight - nothing else fills your mind other that - kill or be killed! Storm Cloud will send forth hundreds of his rogue warriors to rid the Territory of any Paleface encountered.

Badger and Grit drive their mule team relentlessly, pushing the animals to their limit. The big old muleskinner knows of a place to seek refuge and protection from Storm Cloud's brutal braves. Badger heads the wagon straight to Fort Fetterman located in central Wyoming. The large fortification is well fortified and well defended. Army soldiers stationed at the Fort pose a strong enough threat, that War Party braves would not dare attack the military facility. As Badger and Grit enter through the big wood gates of the Fort, the two Traders breath a sigh of relief - knowing they've escaped with their lives!

Secure behind the tall Fort walls, manned by Soldiers with new repeater rifles, they can finally relax; find some Whiskey, and perhaps a friendly game of Poker. As the two men sit at the local Saloon within the massive Fort grounds, Grit leans over and whispers, "Are you gonna tell the soldiers about Dry Gulch?" Badger takes a sip of Whiskey from his glass, and replies, "I will tell them tomorrow. (Takes sip) Right now - I'm busy with this!" Badger holds up his Whiskey glass. Grit nods compliance and settles in for a night of drinking and gambling.

The next morning, the two Traders approach a soldier, and Badger remarks, "Who do I talk to about a burned out settlement?" The soldier points to the veranda at a long wood building, and replies, "The Fort Commander is inside. Tell the Corporal you want to speak with the Commander!" The two men gaze at the long building, and Grit slaps the young soldier's back, "Thank you son!" Badger and Grit walk across the Fort's open Parade Ground, reach the building and step onto the veranda. Badger opens the door, and they both enter inside. The door closes. Once inside, the men face an Army Corporal stationed at his desk. The Corporal gives the two Traders a curious look. Badger remarks, "We'd like to speak with the Fort Commander." The Corporal rises to his feet and enquires, "May I ask what this is about?" The Traders exchange eye contact with each other, and Badger replies in a serious tone, "A burned out settlement - Indian Trouble!" The Corporal's eyes widen and he quickly pivots about and goes into his Superior's Office. Mere seconds later, the soldier returns and comments, "The Commander will see you!" Badger and Grit walk over to enter the Commander's Office. Inside the chamber, the Fort Commander, "Lieutenant Colonel Roxston" sits behind a large wood desk. Framed Military photos line the walls on each side - pictures of West Point Graduates, Army Generals, Washington Politicians, beloved family members, and the United States President - Abraham Lincoln. Colonel Roxston stands up and walks from the desk to greet his two visitors. The Commander remarks, "Good Day Gentlemen! (Pause) What's this I hear about some Indian trouble?" Grit and Badger stand casual, and Badger replies, "Our settlement at Dry Gulch was burnt to the ground! (The Commander eyes him) Indian arrows were everywhere!" The Lt. Colonel enquires, "What about the people?" Grit speaks up, "All dead. Every last one!" Badger satisfies the Commander's next thought, and remarks, "We took our wagon into town 5 hours away - to get supplies. When we returned - our settlement was destroyed - full of burned corpses." Lt. Colonel Roxston puts his hand to his chin to ponder, and remarks, "I've heard stories about an Indian called Storm Cloud - a wild young Chief with a large War Party!" Badger and Grit glance at each other, and Badger comments, "Stories about Storm Cloud are all across the Territory! There are Indian attacks everywhere. (Pause) What's the Army going to do about it?" Colonel Roxston walks over to the wall, looks at the framed photo of President Abraham Lincoln, and responds, "There is a signed Peace Treaty between the Indian Tribes of the Great Plains and our Government in Washington. (Looks at men) As long as the Indian Tribes hold the Peace - there's nothing the Army can do." Grit becomes a bit indignant, "Storm Cloud is attacking everyone across the Plains!" The Commander returns to sit behind his big desk and remarks, "He's a rogue warrior with rogue braves - the Indian Chiefs have told us he represents no Tribe. (Pause) No Tribe - No broken Peace Treaty!" Badger and Grit stand motionless, taking a moment to digest the Commander's last statement. Badger comments, "We've heard enough. Thank you for your time Commander." They leave the Commander's Office, and return to the Fort's watering hole. Badger holds a bottle of Whiskey and pours a shot for Grit and himself, then, the old muleskinner snidely remarks, "The Commander would lock us up if he knew we sold whiskey to Storm Cloud!" They both down their shot of liquor, and Grit comments, "At least we're safe behind the walls of this Fort!" Badger gives his tall lean partner a hard stare, and remarks, "We're only safe as long as nobody knows we were connected to Storm Cloud!"

Out on the rolling grasslands, a long Wagon Train of homesteaders and farmers journey across the Plains. The Thompson-Carter Wagon Train, named for the two Chicago businessmen that organized the venture, left St. Louis, Missouri, and travels west - toward the promise of 40 acres and a chance to put down new roots. The homesteaders are a mixed lot, made up mostly of large and small families with little children, blushing newly weds, old couples, tradesmen, farmers, and new immigrants freshly arrived to America. The Trail Boss, "Sam Fuller", a former Cowboy and Buffalo Hunter, has been leading Wagon Trails on the Oregon Trail for a number of years. For this trip, there are 45 wagons in the group. The long line of buckboards stretch out on the horizon. From high above, the covered wagons form a long white line against the green grass. The people rise with the sun, travel all day and rest at night. In the evening, meals are cooked over an open fire, usually followed by a cup of coffee or tea for the adults. The folks relax with friendly conversation, share stories, or play musical instruments like fiddles, accordions, and guitars. Occasionally, if there's an important event like a Holiday, Anniversary or Birthday, the travellers have a Hoe-Down with lively singing and dancing under the stars. Sam Fuller learned long ago, the wisdom of posting armed guards at various spots to protect the Wagon Train at night. As the Trail Boss looks over his community of travellers fast asleep, Sam feels the burden of having so many lives under his care; that in itself, is the greatest responsibility of a Trail Boss. During the time he's led Wagon Trains west, there's never been any trouble with the Indian Tribes since the Peace Treaty. Finding all is well, Sam Fuller calls it a night and goes to his wagon to get a good night's rest.

The next day, the expedition find themselves on an expanse of flat grassland with gentle rolling hills on both sides. The sky is blue and the temperature is milder than usual, which helps to make the trip more pleasant instead of sweltering under the hot sun. Sam rides his horse at a steady pace as he leads the flock of settlers forward. He looks over his shoulder at the long column of covered wagons trailing behind him. Several men on horses with rifles, ride alongside the pioneer convoy. The Trail Boss halts the procession to make the wagons roll to a stop. He sets his eyes on the horizon ahead and ponders, the wagons have been rolling since sunrise, and the people are tired and likely hungry. Sam Fuller turns his horse around and rides back to the wagons at the front, and remarks, "We'll stop here to get some grub and rest up the animals. Pass it on." The message begins to get passed along from wagon to wagon, and soon, families and individuals climb down onto the ground to stretch their legs and get some provisions. The men, women, and children, stand at their wagons taking care of things, and some folks are moving between wagons to visit. The children like children everywhere take the opportunity to run, play, and have fun. Sam Fuller rides down the line of wagons, greeting folks, and checking to see that all the wagons are okay. He's started this practice years ago, to conduct wagon inspects during stops. Everything is fine, and the Trail Boss rides back to the front. Sam will wait and give time for the people to get a chance to eat, and for the horses and mules to rest up. Sam smiles as he hears the sounds of conversations and children laughing.

**LOUD SCREAMS!  YELLS!  WAR CRIES!**

Sam Fuller looks around in the direction of the sounds. The man sees hundreds of Indian warriors pouring over the hilltops on both sides of the wagon Train. The people could not be caught at a worst time - the wagons stopped - the people scattered - the men with weapons unprepared. Sam bolts his horse and races down the Wagon Train and cries out the alarm, "INDIANS! INDIANS! FORM A CIRCLE!." Terror gripes the people, parents are panicking, their children begin to cry, as the blood-curdling SCREAMS fill the air. Everyone quickly tries to get back on their covered wagons. The people are frantic. The men and women start to drive their teams of horses forward. Sam Fuller rides fast to reach the front wagon. He directs the couple to turn the horse team in a wide arc toward the last wagon. The Trail Boss swiftly scans about - the approaching Indians are far enough away - there's still time to form the Wagon Circle. Sam turns his horse about and speeds alongside various wagons, shouting encouragement, "Move your wagon! Make a Circle!" He watches as the drivers swiftly move to form a circle of covered wagons. Sam continues to ride past the wagons, and shouts, "GET REDY TO SHOOT! STAY BEHIND YOUR WAGON!" The people jump off their wagons and take positions behind the wooden defence. Men and women, and older children, brace with rifles and pistols in hand. The people watch in silent horror as fierce Indian warriors ride toward them.

Storm Cloud had received previous news of the Wagon Train crossing the Plains. His scouting braves reported back on its progress. The rogue Chief picked this location because it is flat and open, with no rocks or trees for protection. Storm Cloud divided his braves so a War Party can attack from each side. With no Whiskey to give his warriors, the young Chief filled them with hatred and lies about the White Man. Fuelled with vengeance and a distorted image of all Whites, War Party braves ride hard at the circle of covered wagons - YELLING and SCREAMING WAR CRIES! Inside the Wagon Circle, Sam Fuller rides his horse by the people as they hunker down at their wagons, "Use rifles for distance. Pistols for close range!" He repeats the instructions until all the families and individuals have heard. The thundering sounds of hundreds of horses and the chilling CRIES of the attacking braves get closer and closer. The Trail Boss grabs his Buffalo rifle from the saddle holster and chambers a bullet, he looks around at his people and yells, "START SHOOTING!" Puffs of white smoke rises from the Wagon Circle as rifles are being fired. POW! POW! POW! The homesteaders aim and shoot their guns at the attackers. The horde of War Party braves fire their bows releasing a torrent of arrows at the wagons - piercing the white covers, and hitting the buckboards all over, making them look like pincushions bristling with feathered arrows. The fierce warriors begin to ride around the wagons firing their rifles and arrows. During the intense battle, many men, women, and children, are killed by War Party bullets and arrows. These were peace-loving settlers unaccustomed to the hostility of battle. On the ground beyond the Wagon Circle, many of Storm Cloud's braves lay on the ground shot dead. Suddenly, the Indian warriors withdraw and ride off to disappear over the hills. Sam Fuller walks about the Wagon Circle inspecting the damage. He is sad as he sees men, women, and children crying as they hold and cradle their lifeless family members - dead fathers, mothers, and children. The Trail Master secretly ponders and figures they've lost half the people. What began as 300 eager souls dreaming of frontier life, has now become a battered group of 150 survivors. Sam Fuller stops beside a wagon where three young children weep uncontrollably as they hug and cradle their dead father and mother. The Trail Master's eyes well up with tears as he looks at the fright and anguish in their young eyes. As he thinks of what kind of solace to offer the siblings, a women from a nearby wagon hastens over to comfort the children. The woman and Sam exchange eye contact, and the lady gently nods her head to indicate she will be there to help. Sam nods and continues his ride to further inspect the harm done. The man gazes around at those who remain alive - they look weary, dazed, angry, and scared. Everyone had heard about Indians attacking Wagon Trains, but that was years ago - no one ever expected this barbaric act. In the lull, Sam raises his voice and calls for a quick meeting, "People! People! Let's gather up!" The homesteaders respond slowly at first, and then quickly move to form a loose huddle in the middle of the drawn wagons. Everyone's eyes are on the Trail Boss. Sam scans their faces and remarks, "For any family wagons that can spare a survivor - we need people to drive any remaining wagons. (Pause) We can't stay here. The Indians will return - we have to move now!" One farmer lifts his arm and asks, "What about our dead? We've got to give them a Christian burial." Sam Fuller understands the man's point of view, however, the reality of frontier life dictate other. The Trail Boss steps close to the man and replies, "If we take time to bury our dead (Looks about) We'll all be dead just like 'em!" He knows it sounds harsh, but the realities of Frontier Life sometimes don't allow for proper civilities. Out in the Wild West, it's, "Live today so you can live tomorrow!" Sam knows the time and effort to bury over a hundred dead bodies will remove any hope of escape and survival. He stands still and looks at the people. Slowly, the truth sinks in and the people move to get ready to depart. Those who are free and able, help to drive some of the abandoned covered wagons. Sam Fuller rides to the front of the line and waits. The survivors steer their horse teams to form a Wagon Train behind the Tail Boss. Sam Fuller looks around and senses all is ready. He waves his hand forward and the wagons pull out to resume their trek across the Plains on the Oregon Trail. Many folks cast a glance back to look at the scattered wagons bristled with arrows, empty and still, with their dead slumped over or laying on the ground.

The convoy of pilgrims race ahead trying to cover lots of ground, seeking to put distance between them and the site where their dead lay. Sam Fuller rides beside the wagons coaxing the drivers to keep the wheels rolling. He knows the further they get away, the better and safer they'll be. The Trail Boss continues to urge the people onward, he doesn't want any stranglers. The Wagon Train has been going at a steady rate, the midday sun is high overhead and the temperature hot. Sam looks at the people - they're tired - the animals are tired. SUDDENLY! RIFLE BLASTS! WAR CRIES! Sam lifts his eyes to sweep the landscape and grabs his rifle. Off a ways back, a large WAR PARTY race their horses straight at them. The Trail Boss turns his horse about and swiftly rides along the column, and yells, "HIGH TAIL IT! INDIANS!" The frightened people take their whips and begin to lash at the horses and mules - CRACK! CRACK! The drivers let out WHISTLES and LOUD YELLS, and shout, "HEY-YAW! GIDDY-UP!" The horse and mule teams jolt forward, with hooves digging into the dirt, and the animals strong legs pulling the loaded wagon faster and faster. As the attacking Indians get closer, Sam Fuller and the settlers start shooting their rifles at them. POW! POW! POW! Bullets take out a number of warriors at the front. The warriors keep coming - YELLING - SCREAMING - hollering WAR CRIES! Women and children in the wagons cling together in fear. Arrows and bullets from the attacking warriors fly in the air at the speeding Wagon Train. By now, the horses and mules are racing full out, their hooves eating up the ground. The drivers begin to have trouble handling the animals, and steering the wagons as the buckboards bounce and jostle about. The wagons are going too fast over the rough ground. To the horror of others, a number of drivers lose control - their wagons veer sideways and flip over to smash on the ground. CRASH! Some wagons bust apart spilling their contents and settlers into the dirt - many of the people are injured. Other wagons land on their side intact - the belongings strewn about, the families vulnerable with no escape. The remaining wagons race onward, the men and women keep firing their guns at the Indians, but it's hard to shoot a moving target when the wagon is tossing to and fro. Sam Fuller looks back - he sees War Party braves kill the families and individuals of the downed wagons. It seems cruel and heartless not to go back to help, but the Trail Boss must press on to keep them racing their wagons to escape the attackers. The sounds of the War Party get closer. The rogue braves are catching up with the wagons, riding alongside to shoot their guns and fire arrows. Some warriors jump from galloping horses onto the covered wagon to attack the driver and people inside. Overpowered and outnumbered, the Wagon Train succumbs to the onslaught and terror. With only five remaining wagons, Sam Fuller and those still alive, make a valiant attempt to speed to safety. Yet, as heroic as it is, the fierce warriors catch up to the remaining few. The Trail Boss pulls out his pistol firing at the braves, killing four. WHOOSH! WHOOSH! Arrows strike his back and chest - he feels the sharp arrowheads inside his body. He fights the pain. As his strength weakens, he watches as the last of the homesteaders are killed by gunshots, tomahawks, knives, and arrows. With his last ounce of strength, the Trail Boss looks to see flickering flames - the War Party burn the wagons and the people inside. On his horse in the distance, Storm Cloud grins wide at the burning wagons and the scattered dead people. Clouds of smoke rise across the landscape - Black smoke from burning wagons that once belonged to 300 homesteaders - men, women, and children.

# CHAPTER TWENTY-ONE

## *The Public Outcry*

The heartbreaking news of the Thompson-Carter Wagon Train reach back east, and it's Front Page News on major Chicago Papers. The slaughter of innocent peace-loving men, women, and children, stirs the anger of the citizens. A large public outcry develops into an organized petition that calls for politicians to do something. The two Chicago financiers, Mr. Thompson and Mr. Carter, the organizers and the fateful Wagon Train, use their wealth and considerable influence to raise public awareness. City and State politicians begin to receive letters and even personal visits, requesting the Government take action to protect families wanting to settle frontier lands. The politicians know the nation will not grow as envisioned unless the American people are free to settle out west. Government officials in Washington meet with Army Superiors to seek a solution. The politicians realize the validity and limits of the standing Peace Treaty that was signed by the Government and the Plains Indian Tribes. The question remains: "What can we do about Storm Cloud and his horde of warriors?" The Politicians and Generals engage in long closed-door meetings, with plenty of heated debates back and forth. Finally, a solution is reached. The Army Generals make the decision to send out limited detachments of Calvary troops to hunt down and punish Storm Cloud and his War Party braves. The reason to utilize limited detachments is give enough soldiers to deal with the renegade threat, while at the same time, the limited force does not break the accords of Peace Treaty. If the Politicians and Generals send in the Army full force, that Military action will break and dishonour the signed Peace Treaty. Military Orders are quickly dispatched to Fort Commanders informing of Washington's decision to send out limited detachments. Troops of

Calvary Soldiers begin to leave Forts to comb the Plains in an effort to find Storm Cloud and his rogue braves. The Soldiers search the grasslands, rugged hills, and forest regions, but to no avail - it's as if the renegade Chief and his wild braves have vanished into thin air.

A column of soldiers from Company "A" out of Fort Carson carefully ride their horses down a valley escarpment heading for the forest below. The Captain saw signs of Indians in the trees below, and decides to investigate. The horses tread their hooves gingerly going down the slope, the animals' instincts have a natural caution. Halfway down the incline, Company "A" soldiers are attacked by War Party braves. Caught in a horrendous position, the column of soldiers face attacking warriors at the front, and in the back. The troops are pinned down with no way to escape, easy targets that are exposed on the escarpment slope, with a drop-off on one side and a rock face on the other. Bullets and arrows rain down as the soldiers attempt to fire their rifles at the front and to the back, all while trying to keep their horses from going over the edge of the escarpment. Rapid fire from the Troop's repeater rifles kill many of the attacking warriors, however, many soldiers and horses are struck with gunfire and arrows. The slope becomes littered with severely wounded or dead soldiers and horses. In the confusion and mayhem, several horse and men fall off the slope to their deaths below. The barrage of gunfire and Indian arrows decimate the Calvary unit, the men of Company "A" continue to fight. Eventually, all that's left are the three remaining soldiers. As two soldiers hold their wounded comrade upright, all three fire their rifles in a valiant effort to defend their position. Bullets and arrows fly through the air to strike them dead. Storm Cloud looks from his vantage point. On the escarpment slope, lays the remains of Company "A", a jumbled bloody mess of slain soldiers and horses, full of gunshots and arrows.

**SCREAMS, YELLS** and **WAR CRIES** echo across the valley!

# CHAPTER TWENTY-TWO

## *Army Soldiers*

Two weeks pass, before Army Scouts bring word back about the tragic end of the Captain and soldiers of Company "A". The General at Fort Carson sends out two columns of soldiers with strict orders to find Storm Cloud. Across the Plains, Indian scouts track the soldiers and report the information to their Chief. The two columns of Calvary soldiers in their blue uniform and yellow handkerchief, visibly stand out traveling on the Plains. The Indian scouts have no problem spotting them, and follow at a discrete distance. Regular reports keeps Storm Cloud continually aware of his enemy's strength and position. At the evening fire, the young Chief talks with Grey Wolf and Running Elk about attack strategy. The recent victory over the Calvary soldiers, and the previous attack on the Wagon Train, have made the rogue warriors feel mighty and invincible against the White Man. The young braves are no longer the innocent youth of the past, now, these young braves have become bloodthirsty warriors, totally dedicated to Storm Cloud's will and ways. No effort is too demanding - no sacrifice too great. In the hearts and minds of the hundreds of warriors, Storm Cloud will make the Indians great once again, all across the entire Great Plains.

The Captain and Major of the two units decide to rest the soldiers for the night beside a small woods located near a small shallow river. Thee will be fresh water for men and horses, and trees for firewood and shade from the heat. The men dismount and the horses are tethered and ties to a secured rope line. While a number of soldiers enter the trees to collect fire wood, others go to the stream to get a refreshing drink of water and to fill their canteens. The two Officers post soldiers to guard and keep watch. Calvary soldiers when traveling in the open wilderness, are accustomed to roughing it, and simply use their saddle as a support to rest or sleep against. The men are happy to get a chance to relax, and some readily doze off oblivious to the others around them. The soldiers that entered the woods return with armloads of wood branches and twigs for the fire. Soon, the Troopers have some fires going around which they can relax, stay warm, and even brew some strong black coffee. The posted sentries have their eyes peeled, as they constantly look about while on guard. Out on the Plains, six hundred yards away, War Party scouts quietly watch the Soldier Camp.

The morning sun peeks over the horizon, as the Army Troop rise and start their day. The soldiers fuel up on cups of coffee and Army rations. The two units get ready to mount up and begin another day of hunting the elusive rogue Chief. The Major and Captain watch the men position their horses to form two columns of soldiers. The Major waves forward, and the units move out to leave their campsite. The Officers lead the troopers in a southeast direction, out over the grasslands toward a distant region thick with sagebrush and saltbush shrubs. A detail of five soldiers ride point to scout and survey what's ahead. The temperature is mild and a slight wind blows over the terrain, the blades of prairie grass bend and flow with the breeze. The two columns ride at a steady rate, the soldiers staying alert as they move over unfamiliar territory. The flat prairie ground changes to become hills and vales filled with saltbush shrubs, sagebrush, and leafy dwarf trees. The Army Officers take their units through the hilly terrain, the soldiers riding in column formation. The five Army scouts ride on the hilltop for better visibility, ready to give out warning should any trouble arise. As the columns of soldiers quietly move along, the silence only broken by the steady sound of hooves digging the ground, and the snorting of horses as they breath. The troops travel at the bottom of a long vale, when - SUDDENLY - Indian arrows strike the five scouts on horseback. The dead scouts fall off their horses.

**LOUD WAR CRIES!**

The Major, Captain, and soldiers alerted by the gunshots and loud War Cries quickly look about. Hundreds of warriors on foot, pour over the crest of the hill on all sides, to descend on the Soldiers at the bottom of the vale. The troopers fire their rifles in all directions at the attacking braves. There is a hail of bullets, hot lead flies through the air on both sides - Indian braves and Army soldiers get killed. The soldiers fire their repeater rifles rapidly, enabling the troops to kill and wound many of the attackers. The Indian warriors have older single shot rifles, the warriors fire once, then have to reload a bullet to fire again. The Major orders the troopers to concentrate their firepower toward the front. The deluge of army bullets decimate the rogue braves at their front position. As a mass of Indian braves drop dead, the Major yells his order, "CHARGE!" The Troopers charge their mounts ahead, breaking their way through the gap created from the dead warriors. The soldiers direct their gunfire at the sides and back position. They bolt their horses up and out of the vale, fleeing the Indian braves on foot. The attacking warriors must run up the hillsides to get their animals. Storm Cloud watches in anger as his warriors waste time and energy, getting back to the crest of the vale to retrieve their horses. The time difference allows the Officers and Troopers to put a good distance between them and their attackers. The Major races his horse all out, his troops following close behind. Ahead, the soldiers see an elevated rock formation, the cluster of big rocks will give the tactical advantage of 'High Ground', from where the soldiers can defend their position to save their lives. Moving swiftly, the soldiers ride up in between the boulders and rocks. There is a space behind the big boulders that's large enough to keep the horses. The Major, Captain, and troopers take firing positions among the rocks and boulders to cover every direction. Now, the soldiers wait for the attack. The Indian warriors cannot to use their Fire Arrows to burn them out. The high rocks give the Troopers better line of sight to shoot their attackers. Storm Cloud and his War Party ride toward the rock formation - the soldiers fire their rifles and warriors in front are shot off their horses. The young Chief lifts his arm and directs his braves to retreat - back out of rifle range. As his War Party anxiously wait, Storm Cloud and his two leaders, study the soldiers' position. The soldiers are protected by the rocks, have a higher vantage point, and their modern rifles can fire bullets a greater distance. For now, the young rogue Chief and his War Party braves are thwarted and stew in anger.

The minutes and hours go by, and still Storm Cloud and his braves have not attacked. The Chief realizes if his fighters attack, the Army's rapid fire will cut down his numbers. Grey Wolf and Running Elk strategize with their Chief - the War Party are not able to get above them like at the escarpment, and they cannot surprise attack from bushes like at the vale, and shooting fire arrows will do nothing except waste the braves' arrows. The Indian leaders agree the only thing they can do is wait the soldiers out until they have no more water and food. Storm Cloud reluctantly agrees to wait in an effort to force the White Man's soldiers to come out. He instructs the braves to set up a makeshift Camp. The War Party braves spread out to find suitable ground to lay low and be ready.

Looking out from the high rocks with their binoculars, the Army Officers see the Indian warriors settled in, and silently keeping their eyes on the soldiers' defensive position. The Major and Captain issue orders to the troops to limit consumption of their canteen water and food rations, and that soldiers are to watch for anyone that disobeys. With discipline and cooperation - the soldiers can hold out for one to two weeks, if necessary. But it will take every trooper to follow the Major's orders, even if they feel thirsty or hungry. The Officers count on the troops' instilled Army discipline to help the warfare tactic work. The minutes give way to hours, which gives way to days. Day One, Two, and Three were taxing, and the soldiers jumped whenever they saw movement by the warriors, but nothing happened. As the days and nights went by, the Troopers found it difficult to fight off thirst and hunger. A soldier caves in to his appetite and devours a good portion of his rations. The trooper is caught and disciplined as a lesson to the others - he is made responsible to clean and store all the droppings from the horses. Not only that, the unfortunate soldier has to sleep beside the manure pile, having to endure the smell and the flies. Aside from the incident, the Officers and the troopers keep up the battlefield strategy. With the rogue warriors watching the soldiers - and the soldiers watching the War Party - it's become a tense drawn-out stalemate!

Back at Fort Carson, when the Major, Captain, and the two Columns never returned after a week, the General immediately sends out two extra Columns from "B" Company as reinforcements. The additional Units are led by a Captain and a Sergeant, and have an Army Indian Scout to help track and guide their search. The Indian Scout has no problem following the direction and the route left by the previous Army Units. The extra Troopers find the campsite near the woods, and begin to trace the trail that leads to the sagebrush and saltbush region. The two Companies stop at the vale, and notice the evidence of a recent skirmish with the telltale evidence of empty bullet casings and Indian arrows on the ground. The Captain and Sergeant order the men to make haste as the Indian Scout picks up their trail. Riding farther into the wilderness area, there's the sound of gunshots - gunfire from repeater rifles. The Troopers know it belongs to their fellow soldiers. The Captain waves the Troopers forward toward the action. As they reach closer, the Captain uses his binoculars to see War Party braves attacking the rock formation, where the Major and his soldiers are returning fire. The Captain signals the Bugler to sound ATTACK and he waves the two Columns forward to attack the War Party from the rear. Storm Cloud and his leaders hear the Army Bugle and turn their eyes to see two Columns of Troopers riding at them with rifles blazing and swords drawn. The rogue Chief knows that his forces can become trapped between the two Army Units, his braves will not stand a chance against rapid rifle fire from the front and at the beck. Storm Cloud raises his arm and waves his warriors to flee. Immediately, the braves jump on their horses and follow Storm Cloud as he rides away from the conflict. As the War Party disappears in the distance, The Major and the soldiers stand to make themselves visible. The Captain, Sergeant, and the reinforcements ride to the base of the rock formation. The Major descends the high ground, and the Captain and Sergeant salute. The Major salutes back and remarks with a big smile, "Sure glad to hear that Bugle and see your troops!" The Captain replies, "We didn't know what we'd find - Good that you and the soldiers are still alive!" The Major looks at his own men, grins and comments, "We're alive all right! - But we sure could use some food and water!" The surviving troopers nod their heads and smile - relieved to be rescued, and happy they'll be free to eat and drink again. After the soldiers are tended to - the four Army Columns make their way back to Fort Carson.

# CHAPTER TWENTY-THREE

## *Beyond Reach*

Storm Cloud and his War Party ride to their hidden Camp, the rogue Chief very upset at having to flee the Army soldiers. Even though he has hundreds of young warriors, the Army's repeater rifles can shoot five bullets for every bullet fired by one of his braves. The retreat was a great blow to his ego, and possibly undermined his leadership among the young warriors, who believe that Storm Cloud is invincible. The Chief's scouts bring word to him that Forts across the territory are sending out columns of soldier to hunt him down. Later at night, around the tepee fire, Storm Cloud, Grey Wolf, and Running Elk talk of the new dangers they face, and how to evade the soldiers. As his two leaders continue to discuss strategy, Storm Cloud remains quiet a long time as he stares at the flickering flames of the fire. Grey Wolf gets his attention and remarks, "My Chief! My Chief! What do you want us to do?" Storm Cloud turns to his close friends and replies, "We will go past the Wilds and make our Camp on "Sky Tower!" Grey Wolf and Running Elk ponder the Chief's decision for a few seconds, then both warriors smile and nod. Running Elk comments, "Storm Cloud is wise and cunning! No soldiers will reach us there!" All three men have a grin of satisfaction at the clever plan.

Storm Cloud and the War Party travel across the lands, careful to avoid any columns of soldiers hunting for them. The large group make their way over the scruffy tundra and journey through the dry parched Wilds, to reach territory that features rock spires and high buttes of various sizes. In the centre of this region is a massive towering butte known to the Indians as "Sky Tower", a giant stone monolith that soars 920 feet high. The geological formation features tall vertical walls of solid rock, with a long wide flat surface on top. The only access is up a steep narrow trail, just enough for one horse; the trail winds its way around the Butte to eventually reach the top surface. The War Party's ascent is slow and time consuming, the trail only allows for them to ride single file. The braves must slowly ride up the winding narrow incline, even for a Plains Indian brave, carefully maneuvering his horse up the trail is a challenge. It takes the better part of an entire day for the large group of warriors to make the trip. Once at the top, Storm Cloud and his force are totally safe - unreachable and untouchable! Unreachable, because the narrow trail is easily defended, the pathway hard and difficult, any approaching soldiers will be killed. Untouchable, because the rogue warriors are beyond the bullets of the repeater rifles. As part of his plan, Storm Cloud has instructed his warriors bring plenty of food, water, and ammunition, for their stay at the top of Sky Tower. Having reached the flat top of Sky Tower, the young Chief and his mass of warriors gaze out across the land far below. Some braves look over the edge, it's a drop of hundreds of feet to the ground below - a fall would be deadly. As they continue to look out from the lofty site, Storm Cloud lifts up his arm and the braves look at their leader. The young Chief sweeps his arm across and remarks, "Up here, where the Hawk flies, we are safe from the White Man! (Looks at braves) No soldiers can touch us here!" As the entire War Party let out resounding YELLS, SCREAMS, and WAR CRIES - Storm Cloud grins and revels that he has outsmarted his foes.

As the various Columns of soldiers criss-cross the landscape, the Army Scout with "B" Company finds tracks left by the renegade braves. The Indian Scout guides the Army Unit over the tundra, through the Wilds, and takes the soldiers to the region with stone towers and rugged Buttes. The Captain and Troopers of "B" Company follow the tracks which lead them to the base of the massive Butte of Sky Tower. The Indian Scout gets off his horse and closely examines the horse tracks at the start of the Trail. The Scout goes a good distance up the passageway and disappears out of sight. Shortly later, the Scout returns and goes to the Captain. The Officer asks, "What did you find?" The Indian Scout glances up the narrow winding trail, then replies, "Storm Cloud and his renegade warriors have gone up to the top - traveling single file." The Captain nods, then turns around in his saddle and orders, "I want a detail of 10 soldiers to go up the trail - Report back what's there!" Nearby, a Corporal picks out nine Troopers for the assignment. The Corporal and his team begin to take their horses up the trail, riding one behind the other. The Captain and his force watch as the troopers get further up the winding passageway, until they disappear from view. The hot sun beats down on the soldiers of "B" Company, as the Captain waits for his troopers to return.

## DISTANT GUNFIRE!

The Captain and the soldiers become alert, and wonder what's happened. After several minutes, seven riderless horses, the Corporal and two troopers come down the trail. Two of the soldiers are wounded - one in the left shoulder, the other with a grazed side. Everyone is eager to discover what took place. The Corporal rides up to his Officer, salutes and reports, "We were a fair distance up the trail - when rogue warriors ambushed us! There was no room to fight, maneuver, or take cover. (Pause) We were sitting ducks, Sir!" The Captain dismisses the Corporal, and rides his horse to where the trail begins - and stares up the restricted passageway for several moments. Suddenly, the Captain spins his mount around and rides to the Sergeant and orders, "Take a detail of twenty men up the Trail on foot. Go as far as you can. Report back!" The Sergeant salutes and immediately rounds up enough soldiers to form the detail. The Captain and the others watch as the Sergeant and his small force go up the trail on foot. Soon, the men are out of sight. Time passes and the soldiers of "B" Company patiently wait for word from their exploratory force led by the Sergeant.

## FAINT GUNFIRE!

The Captain and his soldiers lift their heads and look up at the Trail with anticipation. After a number of minutes, four troopers come down the pathway, one is severely wounded in the stomach. As they reach their comrades, the wounded soldier immediately receives care. The Captain rides over and enquires, "What happened? Where's the Sergeant?" The three troopers exchange eye contact with each other, and one man replies, "The Indians attacked us. The Sergeant was killed helping Private Ryan. (Pause) We're all that's left." The Officer is frozen for a moment, then comments with sadness, "We lost good men today - good soldiers! (Looks at troopers) You get some rest. Dismissed!" The three soldiers salute and leave to join the others. The

Captain lifts his head to look at the very top of the giant Butte. He knows that Storm Cloud has established the perfect battle position - an inaccessible route - a protected stronghold that's beyond reach. The veteran Officer knows that even if he sent up all his men, everyone would eventually be killed. The Captain looks at his men and gives the order, "Mount Up!" The soldiers of Company "B" mount their horses, and the Captain leads his troops from the towering rock fortress. As the Army soldiers ride away into the rugged landscape, the rogue Chief and his War Party braves watch the troopers from high above. Storm Cloud feels confident and smug, because as long as they are at the top of Sky Tower, the soldiers cannot get them.

The Captain and troopers of "B" Company arrive back at Fort Carson. The Captain immediately goes to give his report. Inside the Fort Commander's Office, the Captain salutes the General, and remarks, "We tracked them across the Wilds right to the Mesas. Storm Cloud and his warriors are hold up on top a tall Butte. (Pause) I lost 23 men trying to go up the trail!" The General's eyes widen, he shakes his head and exclaims, "23 of our soldiers!?" The Captain replies, "Yes Sir! It's a sad day for "B" Company!" The General walks to sit down behind his wooden desk and ponders a couple minutes, then he asks the Captain, "What can you tell me about this Butte?" The Captain responds, "It's long, wide, and very high, with sheer rock walls that rise over 800 feet. The only way up is a narrow trail - room for just one horse. I sent two separate details up the trail. (Pause) Only seven returned!" The General stares ahead in quiet thought as he softly drums his fingers on the desktop. The Fort Commander stands and walks over to a large Territory Map on the wall. He motions the Captain to joint alongside him. As they both stand facing the wall, the General puts a finger on the Map and comments, "You say Storm Cloud is here in the Mesa region?" The Captain answers, "Yes Sir! (Touches Map) This is the location of the tall Butte." The General studies the Map's geological features, then he looks at his junior Officer and remarks, "Our Battle Strategy using Column formation cannot apply. If we use Howitzers and Field Cannons - that contravenes the Accords of the Peace Treaty! (Shakes head) We will just have to wait him out!" The General goes back to his desk, sits down, and comments, "That'll be all Captain. Dismissed." The Captain and General exchange salutes, and the Captain leaves the Commander's Office. He stands outside on the shaded veranda, and looks at the soldiers of his Company. He feels a sadness for all the letters he must write to the widows and family back home, regretfully informing them their loved one were killed in action.

Over the next few days, The General at Fort Carson sends letters to the other Forts, reporting on Storm Cloud's Stronghold - and explaining how the Military Commanders' hands are tied by the Peace Treaty. The Army cannot use Howitzers and Cannon to bombard and flush the rogue warriors off the top of the Butte to surrender. News of all this travels to the various Tribes, and it reaches the Shoshone Village. In response, Chief Bear Claw and the Elders call for a Council Fire. Bear Claw, Eagle Feather, Two Knives, Yuji, and Otter, join the Tribe's warriors for the important meeting. When all the leaders and braves have gathered in the central tepee, Chief Buffalo Sky raises his hand to speak, "My Shoshone brothers - Army letters say Storm Cloud and his warriors are at the top of Sky Tower. The Army cannot reach them." All the braves respond to the news with whispered comments and quiet conversation. Buffalo Sky patiently waits as his people digest what they've just heard. The respected Chief lifts his voice for all to hear, "I will go with Bear Claw, Two Knives, Yuji, and Otter, to Fort Carson to speak with the Army General." The assembled warriors react to Buffalo Sky's announcement with head nods and firm-lipped acknowledgement. Chief Buffalo Sky and the Elders smile as the braves begin to beat drums and chant Shoshone Tribal songs of Courage and Victory. The pounding drums and the chanting voices carry out across the village and over the Plains.

Three days later, the Shoshone travelling party arrive at Fort Carson. At first there is some confusion about their presence, until the soldiers learn the Shoshone Chief wants to speak with the Fort Commander. The Corporal guides the Chief and braves into the Commander's Office, where the General greets them. The Commander looks at the visitors and remarks, "What can I do for you?" Chief Buffalo Sky looks at Yuji, and the young man replies, "It's not what you can do for us - But, what we can do for you!" The General is taken back by the reply. He tilts his head as he studies them, and comments with a mild chuckle, "How can you help me?" Yuji makes direct eye contact and responds in confidence, "Storm Cloud is on Sky Tower - You cannot get to him - But we can! (Pause) We can capture Storm Cloud and turn him over to the Army!" The General's eyes light up with intrigue, and he asks, "If the Army can't get to him - how will you?" Yuji exchanges eye contact with Otter, and replies, "Our Ninjans will go up Sky Tower - capture Storm Cloud - and bring him to you!" The Fort Commander remarks, "We lost 23 soldiers trying to go up the Trail. (Eyes group) How will you do better?" Yuji steps closer and speaks firmly, "We will climb up the stone walls of Sky Tower to reach the top." The old Army trooper shakes his head in disbelief, and challenges, "That's impossible! It can't be done - no one can do that!" Yuji exclaims, "Our Ninjans can do it! - And will do it! (Pause) Our Chief wants to offer the Army our help." The General walks over to gaze out the window at the troops outside, he lingers momentarily, then turns about to address the group with a smile, "If what you tell me is true - The Army will give you everything you need to get the job done!" Yuji explains the Commander's words to Chief Buffalo Sky and the others. The Shoshone braves look at the General and nod with understanding. The General approaches Buffalo Sky and extends his hand, and the old warrior offers his hand as well. There in the Commander's Office of Fort Carson, the Army General and Chief Buffalo Sky shake hands in agreement to work together against a common enemy.

# CHAPTER TWENTY-FOUR

## *Ninjans in Action*

Yuji and Otter and the Ninjan braves are on horseback awaiting the others. Chief Buffalo Sky, Bear Claw, Eagle Feather and Two Knives, ride their horses to join them at the edge of Camp. As the two groups meet, Chief Buffalo Sky looks over the assembled Ninjans, and remarks, "You climb where eagles fly. Be silent. Be swift. Bring us Storm Cloud!" Yuji, Otter, and the Ninjans nod their willingness at the leader's charge. Buffalo Sky lifts his arm in the air to wave the group forward. Off the Shoshone and Ninjans ride, away from their village and out over the rolling grassland. They cross the dusty empty Wilds and travel into the Mesa region. The Army General and his troops will meet them at the base of Sky Tower. Chief Buffalo Sky and the warriors ride their mounts with one determined purpose - to bring the rogue Chief to face the White Man's Justice.

The sun is bright and the sky is clear blue, the temperature is already hot. The Shoshone are the first to arrive at the base of the tall rock fortress. Chief Buffalo Sky tilts his head back to look at Sky Tower - his eyes scan the solid rock walls all the way to the top - he notices there are no branches, vines, or roots, to hold onto to support the climb. Yuji and Otter dismount and walk over to the base to inspect the rock surface - they look up the rock wall and see cracks, crevices, thin ledges, and protruding stone details. Otter glances at Yuji and nods with a smile. The rest of the Shoshone and Ninjans dismount, then a couple braves gather the horses and tie them secure a short distance away. Bear Claw, Eagle Feather, and Two Knives, approach their Chief with perturbed expressions. Bear Claw comments, "There are no shrubs, branches, or vines, for our Ninjans to climb! We fear for our brothers!" Eagle Feather adds, "Sky Tower is very high - a fall would mean death!" Chief Buffalo Sky is moved by the concern for their fellow braves. The aged Tribal leader remarks, "Our Ninjas are special warriors. Yuji and Otter told us it can be done!" Bear Claw glances at the others and replies, "We accept your wisdom, great Chief." The veteran Shoshone braves take position beside Buffalo Sky, as they wait for the General and his troops to arrive. A couple hours pass, then Two Knives alerts their attention and points to a cloud of dust on the horizon, "Look! Army soldiers are coming." The Shoshone braves watch as the soldiers come into sight - the General out front leading the column. When the General and soldiers reach the base, the Commander dismounts and walks over and greets Chief Buffalo Sky. The General gazes up at the lofty heights and comments, "We brought over a quarter mile of rope - just like your Ninjans asked. (Peers up) More than enough rope to go up the tower." The Commander pivots about, motions with his hand, and orders, "Captain. Have your men place the rope bundles here (points near Yuji)." The Captain replies, "Yes Sir!", and instructs the soldiers to retrieve the coils of rope from the supply horses at the back of the Column. The troopers carry the coiled bundles and drop the rope near the feet of Yuji and Otter. The General and Buffalo Sky watch as Yuji and Otter inspect the bundles of lines. Yuji looks at the General and nods with a smile, "Thank You General! The ropes are good and strong!" As Otter lays out the rope in separate bundles, Yuji calls the Ninjans over. The Army Soldiers and the Shoshone braves observe as the Ninjans lay out the lengths of rope, then securely tie the rope ends together with strong intricate Ninjan knots to form a very long rope - enough rope to reach the top of Sky Tower. To prepare for the climb upward, the Ninjans bring out climbing apparatus - each Ninjans will wear a short metal spike on one foot, and a short metal claw on one hand. The metal spikes and claws will help the Ninjans to scale the rock surface. The sharp metal points will lodge into cracks and crevices, and hold onto the ledges and rock details of the tower wall. With the free hand, the team of Ninjans will grab, hold, and manoeuvre the rope as they climb. The Army soldiers have never ever seen Ninjans before and are thoroughly fascinated by the appearance and their weaponry. Each Ninjan is dressed in an all black outfit with the Ninjato and Katana sword in sheaths at the back, along with a Bow and Arrows. A tomahawk, knife, and a black leather pouch are attached at the waist. The black head cover decorated with Tribal beads and feathers, masks their face and only reveals their eyes.

The Ninjans look fierce, menacing and deadly. The Ninjan group work quickly together to ensure the climbing rope is proper and secure. Yuji and Otter stand ground level at the base of Sky Tower and gaze upward. The two Ninjan Masters have an air of confidence, knowing that their tough specialized training has prepared them for such a task. Yuji knows that Sky Tower has given Storm Cloud a false sense of security because he's out of reach of the Army. However, the arrogant young Chief isn't aware the Ninjans can reach him - even at the very top of Sky Tower!

With the end of the rope tied over his shoulder, Yuji is the first to lead the climb. He grabs a ledge with his fingertips, while he puts the toe of his boot into a wide crack to lift himself off the ground. Next, Yuji reaches up to place his fingers into a wide crevice as he puts his foot on a rock detail for support. Upward Yuji climbs carrying the rope with him. Other Ninjans follow in like manner, carefully and skillfully maneuvering up the rock face. As the Shoshone and the Army soldiers watch, the black-clad Ninjans cling like insects to the rock surface. Otter joins in to lead the second portion of the climbers. Slowly and methodically, the group of Ninjans scale the stone walls of Sky Tower, moving steadily toward the top. Halfway up the tall Butte, Yuji looks out from the dizzying height without any fear; his body is fit, his hands and feet are strong, his eyes sharp, his mind alert - his only focus is to securely cling to the rock surface by any means possible. He lowers his eyes at the long line of black figures below him that await his next move. The Ninjan Master spots a crevice and stretches to grab hold, as he puts his foot against a ledge to push himself higher. Aside from a little wind and the hot temperature, the day is just right for such rock climbing. The years of tough Martial Arts training has given the Ninjans' hands a vice-like grip, and made their legs and feet - strong and flexible. All the previous Ninjan training now allows for this moment, where men scale the soaring rock face of Sky Tower to the amazement of their comrades below. At one stage of the climb, the Ninjan ahead of Otter loses his footing and his boot slips. Otter swiftly reaches his arm to garb the boot heel to give support. As Otter strains holding against the extra weight, the Ninjan in front quickly lifts his foot to find another anchor point for support. The man looks at Otter with an expression of deep appreciation, then resumes his upward climb. The foot with the metal spikes and the hand with the metal claw prove invaluable, enabling the Ninjan warriors to lodge in cracks, cling onto thin ledges, and hold secure on the rock details of the Butte's stone wall. By now, Yuji is very close to the top. He stops to listen for any voices or footsteps from War Party braves. There is nothing. Yuji reaches his hand to grip the edge of the top surface and slowly pulls himself up eye-level to peer about. No one is there - no sentries or War Party braves. The Ninjan Master quickly gets up onto the top and crouches low to help conceal his outline. Almost immediately, the next Ninjan reaches the top and moves to lay flat on the rock. Like clockwork, a steady stream on Ninjans reach the top and fan out to lay low to make themselves less noticeable. Soon, all the Ninjans are gathered at the top of Sky Tower. The massive Butte that is both wide and long, with alternating steps and levels. The location where the Ninjans ascended is empty with no War Party braves are around. Otter and a couple Ninjans quietly pull up long sections of line until the entire climbing rope is retrieved and strategically stored nearby. The Ninjans quickly huddle and Yuji gives instructions, "Otter and I will capture Storm Cloud. Smoke bombs for cover - Explosives for confusion. We meet here to go back down!" All the Ninjan warriors nod - everyone understands. Yuji waves his hand - instantly the Ninjans swiftly sprint across the top of the Butte, moving toward the elevated step before them. They reach the Step and Yuji lifts his head to peer what lays in front. He sees clusters of tepees and makeshift canvass shelters where the rogue warriors sleep and find rest in the shade. Yuji was right about the false sense of security, because Storm Cloud placed no guards or sentries across the spacious top surface. That mistake allowed the Ninjans to climb Sky Tower and move freely across the top surface to reach the mountaintop Camp. As a defence, Storm Cloud has placed groups of braves along the narrow upward trail. The warriors are more than enough to fight and destroy any soldiers or intruders. The rogue Chief has assembled his War Party at the top of the Trail - close and ready for any attack or action!

Yuji and Otter sneak through the empty tepees and shelters, looking for Storm Cloud's tepee, while keeping their eyes peeled for any braves. Midway in the cluster of tepees is one tepee that has a War Lance resting against the front entry. The War Lance can only belong to Storm Cloud. The two Ninjans hurry back to join the hidden Ninjans. A Ninjan asks Yuji, "What is our next move?" Yuji looks at the Shoshone brave and replies, "We will move just before dawn - Otter, myself, and some others will steal into the Camp to capture the rogue

Chief. The Ninjan brave nods. For the time being, the troop of Ninjans hunker down out of sight below the stone ledge. They patiently wait through the afternoon, the cold night, until just before the break of day.

The sun has yet to appear over the horizon, the Camp and tepees are filled dark shadows. Any warriors moving about are simply darken figures, their features unrecognizable. Yuji, Otter, and a select few, swiftly move with stealth going through the dwellings, until they stand outside the Chief's tepee. Otter quietly opens the entry flap, and instantly the Ninjans dart inside. Storm Cloud is stretched out sleeping, and attempts to rise. Otter and others quickly grab the rogue leader and hold him tight, while Yuji blows black powder in Storm Cloud's face, the Ninjan powder goes into his nostrils and immediately knocks him out. As four Ninjans guard outside; Yuji, Otter and two others lift their limp unconscious quarry out of the tepee, and quietly carry him away from the Camp, heading toward the section they climbed up. Reaching the ascent area, Yuji and Otter tightly bind Storm Cloud's arms and legs, hands and feet. The rogue Chief looks almost like an Egyptian mummy wrapped with some much rope. At the edge of the surface, four Ninjans carefully position the silenced captive, while Yuji, Otter and two Ninjans securely hold the rope that will lower their prisoner to the ground below. Yuji, Otter and the two men, grip the rope and slowly and methodically, lower Storm Cloud's body further and further down the rock wall. All is well - until!

**LOUD SHOUTS! ANGRY VOICES!**

The Ninjans turn to see angry War Party braves led by Grey Wolf and Running Elk, racing their way. Yuji yells the order, "Smoke bombs and Exploding Arrows!" The Ninjans reach into their side pouches and throw Smoke Bombs, and other Ninjans fire Exploding arrows above the oncoming warriors. POOF! POOF! BANG! That section on top of Sky Tower becomes dense with smoke, making it impossible to see. Thick clouds of smoke blind the attacking warriors. The Exploding arrows frighten and disorient the rogue braves. Attempting to flee in the confusion, a number of the War Party braves run off the top, and fall screaming to their death. Grey Wolf shouts to his warriors, "Stay still! - Go no further! We fight blind - we walk blind." For the few braves that got through the smoke, the Ninjans overpower them with Martial Arts. Yuji waves another Ninjan to hold the rope in his place.

He peers over the edge to see how far down the body is. The bundled captive is close to ground level. With a few more release of the rope, Storm Cloud's body comes within reach of Bear Claw, Eagle Feather, and Two Knives. The Shoshone warriors grab the body and carry it off to the side, and post Indian braves to guard the unconscious prisoner. The Army General and his troops are thrilled to see Storm Cloud securely bound and in their presence. At the top of the tall Butte, Yuji brings out a large thick metal nail and a hammer from a Ninjan's pouch. The Ninjan Master places the strong thick nail into a crack on the top surface, and forcefully pounds the nail deep into the rock. The big metal nail is securely anchored into the stone. Next, Yuji grabs the end of the climbing rope to tightly wrap and tie the rope secure to the large nail. He and Otter tug on the rope - the nail holds rock solid. While thick smoke continues to hang in the air between the Ninjans and the War Party, Yuji motions for the Ninjans to hold onto the rope and descend. Descending by rope is quick and fast. Soon all the Ninjans have reached the ground - only Yuji and Otter remain on top. The smoke begins to clear and a few of the War Party braves race toward them. Yuji remarks to Otter, "Go down the rope my brother - I will quickly follow." Otter nods, grabs hold of the rope and swiftly lowers, going down the tower wall. Suddenly, five rogue braves reach Yuji and surround him with knives and tomahawks. Their faces full of anger and hatred. They attack! As the braves swipe their sharp knife blades and swing menacing tomahawks, Yuji dodges and ducks the attacks from all directions. The Ninjan Master pivots to send out a devastating round-house kick to knock out a brave. He turns to release a flurry of powerful punches that drops two other attackers. The two remaining warriors lunge forward with knives extended. Yuji grabs an arm to forcefully flip one brave hard against the rock to disable him. Yuji kicks the knife out of the last attacker's hand, and pummels him with powerful blows - the brave crumples to the rock surface. Yuji takes a breath and looks as the smoke begins to lift - he races to the edge, quickly grabs the rope, and descends swiftly in what could look as a free fall. Yuji lets the weight of his body carry him swiftly down the long rope. He looks at the ground approaching and he jumps to land safe and sound. Noise and shouts from high above cause the Shoshone and the soldiers to look up. A number of War Party braves attempt to climb down - a reckless and foolhardy move by young inexperienced braves. The Ninjan Leader calls for a lit torch. Yuji lists his arm to cut the rope just above his head - then he touches the flames of the burning torch to the hemp rope. The fibres of the rope ignite, and soon the rope is burning with flames creeping upwards toward the top. The War Party braves begin to climb back up and stand at the top staring down in a rage.

Yuji, Otter and the Ninjans walk over beside Chief Buffalo Sky, the Shoshone, and the General. Before them on the ground, is Storm Cloud bound and tied with intricate Ninjan knots. The rogue leader still unconscious from the effects of the black powder. The General turns to Buffalo Sky and shakes the Chief's hand, the Commander turns his gaze to the Ninjans. The General remarks, "If I didn't see it with my own eyes, I would not have believed it - What you did was remarkable. Truly remarkable!" Yuji, Otter and the Ninjans bow respect to the Commander. As the Shoshone watch, soldiers place the bound captive over the back of a horse. Surrounded by a company of armed soldiers to guard the rogue Chief, the General gives the order, "Company - Move Out!" The Army General and the soldiers of Company "B" take away their prisoner. Storm Cloud will face the White Man's Justice! Chief Buffalo Sky, the Shoshone, Yuji and the Ninjans, mount their horses and ride away from Sky Tower - heading home toward tribal lands and their family tepees.

# CHAPTER TWENTY-FIVE

## *Chains of Defeat*

The column of soldiers cross the sagebrush tundra and the bleak Wilds, all the while keeping their eyes open for any War Party braves attempting to rescue their prisoner. The troopers ride over the rolling grasslands and eventually reach Fort Carson. The Fort's big wooden gates swing open to allow the men of Company "B" to enter the Military grounds. The soldiers inside salute the General as he rides by. The troopers take their horses to the staging area and dismount. The General looks at the Sergeant and orders, "Place the prisoner in chains and put him in the Stockade!" The Sergeant salutes, pivots about and directs two soldiers to assist with the command. By this time, the effects of the black powder have worn off and Storm Cloud is awake and alert. He attempts to struggle free but the Ninjan knots hold him secure. With armed guards standing by, the Sergeant and the two soldiers lift the rogue warrior off the horse and stand him on the ground. The rebellious brave looks around with a defiant stare. As rifles are pointed at the prisoner and the ropes cut away, soldiers shackle Storm Cloud's hands and feet. The strong chains restrict his movement. The Sergeant motions for a Squad of soldiers to escort the prisoner to the Fort Stockade. To move, Storm Cloud has to shuffle his feet in short strides, the chains limit his leg movement. The prisoner moves slowly across the parade ground toward the Stockade. Once inside the building, Storm Cloud lifts his eyes to see a large metal cage with steel bars and a thick cement floor. The Sergeant unlocks and swings opens the metal door, then stands to the side. The soldiers place Storm Cloud in the Prisoner Cell, then quickly exit. The Sergeant closes and locks the thick metal door. CLICK! He orders two soldiers to watch and guard the prisoner. Storm Cloud tries to move his arms apart, but cannot, the chains permit only basic movement. There in the Prisoner Cell surrounded by strong steel bars, the feared bloodthirsty Chief of a fierce War Party; now, stands in defeat, fettered in iron chains, no longer the threat or menace he once was. Stripped of his Chief's War Bonnet and rogue warriors, Storm Cloud looks pathetic and humiliated, bound in chains. When all is taken away, the rogue troublemaker is nothing more than a young brave bound in chains, soon to appear in a Judicial Court, and face the White Man's Justice.

One month later, a crowd of people pack the frontier Courtroom. People from across the Plains have gathered to witness the important Trial - Ranchers, Farmers, Homesteaders, and Townsfolk. Reporters from out east are also present to record and telegraph the events back their big city Newspapers. The Courtroom is filled with chatter as folks anticipate laying their eyes on Storm Cloud and observing the Trial. At the front, bound in chains is Storm Cloud, guarded by four armed soldiers. The tension in the room so great, one could cut it with a knife. There is a small commotion in the back as more spectators try to crowd in to see the proceedings. Suddenly, a door at the front of the chamber opens, "Judge Thaddeus Collins" enters to climb the steps and takes his position behind the Bench. The Judge strikes the Gavel, and remarks in an authoritative voice, "Court is in Session!(scans the people) Everyone please be quiet." The elderly man with curly grey hair and round wire frame glasses, opens a docket and reads through the papers. The Judge looks at a Bailiff, and the man quickly utters, "Will the Prisoner rise." Storm Cloud sits uncooperative. The Judge nods to two soldiers behind the rogue Chief, and they grab his arms and hoist him to his feet. The Courtroom buzzes with muffled conversation. Judge Collins pounds the gavel, "Quiet in the Courtroom!" The people cease talking. Judge Collins peruses the docket, then clears his throat - AHEM! The elderly man looks at the defiant young brave in front of him and remarks, "The State of Wyoming finds the prisoner Guilty of - Cattle Rustling, Murder of Cowboys, Burning Ranches, Homesteads, a School House, and a small town." The Judge peers over his spectacles and continues, "Killing Army soldiers, Attacking and Killing Settlers of the Thompson-Carter Wagon Train, inciting and leading young Indian braves in Rebellion, (Pause) and buying and consuming illegal Whiskey!" All eyes are on Storm Cloud as he stands stoic and silent. Judge Collins admonishes the prisoner, "Do you understand these Charges? (Pause) Do you understand English? How do you plead?" The people in the chamber are hushed with anticipation, the reporters from out east frantically scribble down the proceedings. Storm Cloud lifts his head in a haughty manner and replies, "I know the White Man's tongue. I understand your words (he scans the gallery) Storm Cloud is a War Chief - proud of all I have done against the Paleface!" The Courtroom is aghast! As the young warrior stares ahead, Judge Thaddeus Collins remarks in a firm judicial tone, "By your own admission and words, I find you GUILTY of these crimes against the People of Wyoming, and these United States! I hereby sentence you to **Death by Firing Squad**, (Pause) in the meantime, you will be transferred by train to a Military Prison on the east coast - far away from these lands! Judge Collins pounds the gavel BANG! - then remarks, "Take the prisoner away!" Immediately the soldiers take Storm Cloud out the side door. The entire Courtroom becomes full of commotion as reporters shout questions at the Judge, and people burst in lively conversation and comments about the spell-binding Trial. As people file out of the room, one Rancher turns to another Rancher and comments, "Finally - Justice!"

The following week, a black locomotive spewing dark grey smoke chugs up the tracks and stops at the Railroad Station. The big locomotive lets out a burst of steam that temporarily engulfs the wood platform in a cloud. This transport is a Military Train filled with soldiers and fitted with newly manufactured Gatling guns mounted on top the rail cars. As the train parks at the Station to await its important prisoner, soldiers with rifles take position on both sides of the track. An Army Captain stands next to the Prisoner Car outfitted with bars on the widows and a large steel cage inside. Soon a detail of soldiers brings someone bound in shackles toward the Captain. The Sergeant of the detail, salutes the Officer and remarks, "The Indian prisoner is ready for transport!" The Captain salutes and replies, "Place him inside the metal cage, lock and chain the door secure." The Sergeant salutes and responds, "Yes Sir!" The soldiers lift the man up onto the Prisoner Car and place him inside the empty metal cage. The Sergeant secures the steel door, and wraps it with a steel chain and locks it. The Sergeant looks at the captive - the prisoner looks tired and weak, and keeps his head bowed staring at the floor. With the Army prisoner onboard, the Captain orders the posted guards to return to their positions on board. The Captain waves and the Engineer pulls back the lever and the locomotive begins to turn its big wheels to slowly pick up speed. As the Engineer Assistant stokes the roaring fire in the Boiler with more wood, the engine builds up more power making the train go faster and faster. In a matter of minutes, the Military Train is chugging along headed for the east coast. Inside the Prisoner Car, Storm Cloud lifts his head to get a glimpse out the window at the passing terrain. The rugged landscape was a place he once ruled and reigned as the brash young Chief of a mighty War Party. As scenes of the wilderness fly by the open window, the defeated warrior lowers down to sit cross-leg in the cell. Gone are the SHOUTS, SCREAMS and WAR CRIES - there's only the rumbling of train wheels on steel rails, the clanging of the Box Cars, and the steady sound of the chugging locomotive, as it takes him toward the east coast to his sealed fate!

# CHAPTER TWENTY-SIX

## *Young Warriors Go Home*

The young braves that left their Tribal villages are lost and without direction. Grey Wolf and Running Elk step into the power vacuum to seize control snd take charge. Although the two warriors were Storm Cloud's junior lieutenants, the hundreds of braves that remain in the War Party, fail to submit to their leadership. Without their rogue Chief to untie them, soon, the War Party splinters into various Tribal groups with their own allies. The once united mass of young braves has now become rival factions with different agendas. Self-appointed leaders arise, challenges are made, and fights break out. Grey Wolf and Running Elk watch as their mighty force of fierce warriors, turn into bickering competitive groups trying to usurp dominance. The tension and confusion becomes too much and the War Party dissolves into a memory, as the different groups of braves begin to return to their Tribal lands. The young bucks head out in every direction of the compass, seeking to go home to the Chiefs and Elders they had run away from. When all the others have departed, Grey Wolf and Running Elk take the handful of braves still loyal, go North - to where rumours are told of good hunting and fishing grounds.

At Indian Villages across the Plains, young braves return to make amends and face their Tribe's discipline for running off. Many of the boys that run off, now return a young men and experienced warriors. The fathers and mothers are glad to see their sons return home. Across the different Tribes, Council fires burn as Chiefs and Elders discuss how to receive and treat the runaways. The people cannot forget the terrible damage caused by Storm Cloud; nor, lose sight of the fact Storm Cloud had a powerful sway over those that flocked to him. The rogue warrior poisoned the hearts and minds of the young braves. Now, that Storm Cloud is in Military Prison, and the War Party no more, the returning braves can see the error of their ways. The Chiefs and Elders, the parents and the people, all know that it will take good example and instruction. The young men will eventually learn and mature to become fine braves in their Tribal Village. The process will simply take time, patience, and understanding, to undo the wrong and replace it with good ways to live Indian life.

In the Shoshone Camp, the young braves that ran off, now return with regret for their actions, and embarrassment that they were deceived by Storm Cloud. At the Council Fire, the young braves stand before Chief Buffalo Sky, the Elders, and the lead warriors. Eagle Feather studies the braves and comments with concern, "What if their hearts are still dark?" Two Knives exclaims, "These braves rode in the War Party!" Chief Buffalo Sky looks intently at the young men, then remarks, "In the forest, the big tree overshadows the little trees - taking all the sunlight. If the big tree falls, the little trees can grow properly in the sunlight." Bear Claw and the other leaders nod at their Chief's wise words. Buffalo Sky continues, "These stood in the shadow of Storm Cloud as he blocked the sunlight. He is gone! Now, these young trees (points to braves) are free to grow to be healthy and strong - to become better braves!" The Elders and the Warriors nod their heads as they agree. Chief Buffalo Sky lifts his arm and speaks loud and clear for everyone to hear, "Bear Claw and Eagle Feather will teach these young braves. Yuji and Two Knives will train them to form character. When all is done - these young men will become fine Shoshone braves. (Turns to leaders) Let us allow the young trees to grow!" The assembled warriors let out YELLS and VICTORY CRIES to celebrate the Chief's decision.

# CHAPTER TWENTY-SEVEN

## *The Great Request*

Life on the Plains begins to return to life as they knew it, as farmers, ranchers, and townsfolk, resume their normal routines and daily activities. Cattle freely graze on pasturelands, folks visit town to shop and get supplies, and farmers plant their crops without fear. Everyone wants to put the tragic days of the rogue warriors in the past, and move on to build better days. In the Tribal Villages throughout the Great Plains, there is peace and tranquility, children play outside tepees, braves hunt and fish, the women prepare and sew buckskin garments, and Tribal leaders share stories around Council Fires. All is well!

But, out on the wide grassland, a rickety wooden wagon rolls along pulled by four mules. Holding the reins and driving the team is a big man with scruffy beard wearing soiled unkept clothes. Badger lifts his arm to snap the whip - CRACK! The driver yells out, "Move it you ugly critters!" The mules tug and pull all the harder. The old muleskinner turns to Grit, his old business partner and travel companion, and remarks with a sneer, "It's taken a while - but we're in business again!" The tall skinny man replies, "That Poker Game was so close - I wasn't sure you'd win!" Badger throws his head back with a big LAUGH, and boasts, "I had the cards up my coat sleeve - just waiting - waiting for the Pot to get big!" Grit quips, "All the money you won got us back in business - Mules, Wagon, (Points) and Whiskey!" The two Traders break out LAUGHING as Badger steers the wagon over the terrain. Their destination is an Indian Village where the two will sell their illegal cargo. Badger befriended an Indian brave and used his influence to arrange a visit to the Indian Camp. The old

Trader will use the same strategy he used with the wild young Chief - Badger will give away plenty of free samples of Whiskey to the people. For Badger, it doesn't matter who he gives the liquor to - men, women, young, old - even children. In the Trader's mind, the more people that crave and want Whiskey - the better! The wagon rolls steady through the day until the late afternoon. Badger and Grit see the tepees of the small Indian Village, and prepare to meet the brave they befriended, having given him trinkets and a stolen Army repeater rifle.

There is a stir among the people as the two White Men drive the wagon into the Indian Village. The brave who is their contact greets them, grabs the bridle and leads the mules to stop outside the Chief's Tepee. This Tribe, the "**HOWATAKAS**", a tiny Tribe compared to the others. The Chief and Elders want their Tribe to become more prominent, and welcome Badger's promise to give them repeater rifles, just like the White Man has. Part of the deal includes buying the Trader's Whiskey. The Howataka Chief and braves gather at a Council Fire where Badger and Grit present two more repeater rifles and five barrels of Whiskey. The Chief enquires how much is the price? The big old muleskinner uses the brave as an interpreter and replies, "Three bags full of the small yellow rocks!" The Chief announces to the assembly the details of the transaction, and chatter breaks out across the meeting place. The Tribal Leader lifts up his arm and the chatter stops. The Chief looks at the two Traders and nods - then motions with his hand - and an older warrior brings three leather pouches to the front and hands the bags to Badger. The old Trader opens a drawstring and sifts his fingers through the gold nuggets in the pouch. He closes the drawstring, looks at the Chief and Elders with a smile. Grit brings out the two repeater rifles that were wrapped in a blanket, and presents the guns to the Chief. The Howataka Chief is fascinated with the modern rifle, closely examining the mechanics and details. The old warrior stands to his feet and holds ip the repeater rifle with a big smile. The attending braves break out in YELLS, CRIES, and VICTORY SHOUTS! The Chief gestures and nearby braves remove the cover of the first Whiskey barrel. The Indian Chief and Elders peer in at the amber coloured liquid. A brave dips a hollowed gourd ladle into the barrel to scoop up the strange liquid that moves like water. He gives the gourd ladle to the Chief to take a sip - the Chief COUGHS and gets wide-eyed! The warriors in the room begin to comment aloud. Everyone watches the Chief for any further reaction. The Chief hands the gourd ladle to a nearby warrior and he drinks - his face contorts and he shakes his head. By now, the entire tepee is buzzing with talk and excitement at the Tribe's leaders sampling the new liquid. The Chief dips the ladle into the barrel to gather more of the 'golden water'. The aged brave gives a drink to one of the elders. The man takes a gulp, then puts his hand on his throat - AHHHHH!   The novelty of the taste experience has some braves standing on their feet out of curiosity and to get a better look. Badger and Grit knows from prior experience what comes next, and watch closely. The Chief, Elder, and warrior, exchange eye contact and sport big grins - they're feeling the effects - a warmth inside their body, an urge to taste more, and an unexplainable sense of power. The Howataka Chief looks at Badger, nods and smiles. Badger and Grit know they're in business - there'll be plenty more trips to the Indian Village to supply the growing desire for more Whiskey! As the braves in the tepee begin to pry open the other barrels, the two Traders exit the structure and climb up onto the wagon. Badger grabs the whip's wood handle, pulls back his arm and snaps the long leather cord - CRACK! The mules lunge, their hooves digging into the dirt, their strong stubby legs pulling the wagon forward. Badger and Grit leave the Village - behind them are the sounds of REVELRY, SHOUTING, and INDIAN CRIES!

The two Whiskey Traders bring a supply every month. Over six months, things drastically change in the tiny Indian Village. Braves, and even Squaws, can be seen passed out, quarrels erupt in families between husband and wife, children are left unguided, and fights break out among young braves. The little Tribe has embraced big trouble. Whiskey is a powerful substance - it can be poured over an injury to sterilize the wound, it can also be consumed to the stage people are intoxicated and cannot function. European nations have taken centuries to learn to live with Alcohol and liquor. Over time, norms and social etiquette were developed to govern the manufacturing and consumption of "Spirits". However, to the Native Indian Tribes of the Great Plains - Whiskey is a new, powerful, and greatly unknown. The Tribes have not had the time, experience, or wisdom, to properly handle such a substance. Like any potent ingredient - it can be used for good - or be used for harm. Badger and Grit have no trouble with any harm done by introducing Whiskey to the Indian Tribes. In the minds and hearts of these two Traders, they create the demand - bring the supply - and reap the rewards - Gold!

* * *

News travels fast, and other tribes hear of the Howatakas being exploited by the greedy Traders. The other Tribes feel a sadness for the small peaceful tribe. Once known as a gentle people that lived in harmony, the Howataka Camp is full of strife and discord. Families argue, young braves are rebellious and disrespectful to Elders, Tepees and daily chores are neglected. It has become a community of drunkards ruled by the thirst and influence of alcohol. Warriors dress sloppy, Elders drink during the day, and children cry as parents fight. It was a sad day when Alcohol was introduced to the Howatakas without any guidance, rules, or control. Water is good and essential for life - But too much water can make one drown.

Travellers from other Indian Tribes visit the Shoshone Camp, and share the reports of what has happened to the Howatakas. Chief Buffalo Sky and the Elders call for a Council Fire. The night of the meeting, Chief Buffalo Sky stands before the leaders and warriors, "My Shoshone brothers - my heart is heavy and my spirit cries for the Howatakas. A gentle people have become a troubled people." The leaders and the warriors nod. Bear Claw speaks aloud, "The Traders give Whiskey to the Howatakas (Pause) as they did with Storm Cloud." Eagle Feather asks, "What can we do?" The tepee is silent as the warriors ponder the question. Buffalo Sky glances at Yuji and Otter, then he addresses the assembly, "We will send Yuji, Otter and our Ninjans to help!" Smiles come across the leaders and warriors' faces - heads nod in approval. The large central tepee is filled with SHOUTS and VICTORY CRIES!

The wagon wheels roll and clunk over the rocky ground, as Badger and Grit are travelling to deliver their monthly supply of Whiskey. The sun beats down on the sand, the air is hot and dry. Grit brings the Whiskey bottle to his lips and takes a sip - then wipes his lips, and remarks, "AHHHH! This stuff is good! - Not like the cheaper stuff we give them." LAUGHS! Badger glances over at his partner and replies with a grin, "They can't tell the different. We'll keep it that way!" Both men sneer at Badger's comment.

**SUDDENLY! BLACK ARROWS!**

Badger quickly pulls on the reins to stop the mules. The Traders are surprised and shocked! Their wagon is peppered everywhere with long black arrows. The two Traders look in front and don't know what to make of it - they've never seen such a thing. Figures dressed from head to toe in black clothing - black sword handles and bows and arrows, protrude from their back, black tomahawks, knives, and leather pouches, hang from the waist. The figures in black look frightening and mysterious. The black riders sit on their mounts watching the two men in the wagon. Badger and Grit strain to look, but they can only see human eyes staring back with a cold gaze. The only details that offer any clue are the Tribal beads and feathers attached to the raven hoods. A black rider in the centre of the group, Otter, moves his horse out from the others and stops directly in front of the wagon. Otter declares to the two Traders, "You will not sell any more Whiskey to this Indian Tribe!" Otter gives a slight motion with his hand, and black arrows strike the buckboard between the men's shins. Grit GULPS! Otter continues, "You will not sell Whiskey to any Indian Tribe. (Pause) If you do - we will hunt you down and punish you!" Badger and Grit exchange glances. Otter brings his horse close so he is right beside Badger, and remarks, "Leave you wagon - Go! (Cold Stare) If you stay - you die!" The two men jump off the buckboard, land in the dirt and start running away. Other Ninjans unhitch the mules and slap their backside - sending the mules free to roam the wilderness. Otter turns to a Ninjan and comments, "Bring torches - burn everything!" There in the middle of sand and sagebrush, Otter and his group of Ninjans watch the wagon and barrels of Whiskey burn - an intense inferno with flames shooting high. A Ninjan rider reports back to Otter, "The two bad men are still running!" Otter and the rest wear a triumphant smile.

Yuji and his group of Ninjans, slowly ride into the Howataka Village. The Ninjans are sad to see passed out braves, tepees in shambles and disrepair, and children wandering around crying. Yuji and the others bring their horses to halt at the large tepee in the centre of the Camp. Bye this time, anyone sober in the Camp has gathered out of curiosity. A small group of Howataka warriors cluster and stand proud in a defensive posture. Yuji smiles inside his heart at discovering there are still sober Howataka warriors ready to defend their Tribal Village. Out from the large tepee steps the Howataka Chief. The older warrior studies the black riders before his eyes, then he enquires, "If you going to robe us - We are a small Tribe and have nothing of value." Yuji dismounts and removes his head covering. The Chief recognizes Yuji as a Shoshone brave. YUji steps close and comments, "Do not fear Great Chief - we do not come to steal - we are here to give!" The Chief scans his eyes around the dishevelled Camp and replies sadly, "What will you give us (Pause) more Whiskey?" Yuji motions his arm and the other Ninjans dismount and gather beside him. As the Ninjans remove their hoods and gaze at the Howataka Chief, Yuji remarks, "We give hope! We are here to help restore your Camp, so that once again, the Villagers can be proud Howataka people." The Chief's eyes become watery at hearing such encouraging words. The old warrior turns and lifts the flap of the tepee entrance and invites, "Let us sit around the fire and talk more." As the few Howataka braves watch, Yuji and the Ninjans enter the Chief's tepee, where inside, Yuji will speak of the ways the Ninjans can help.

Over the succeeding days and weeks, the Howataka Chief begins to see the benefits and wisdom of having the Ninjans live among his Tribe. Yuji and the Ninjans prepare special herbal teas and elixirs to help cleanse the system and bring life and vitality back to the people. Otter and other Ninjans go out daily to hunt and fish, bringing game to the campfire where the Ninjans cook hearty meals for the men, women, and children. Going days and weeks without alcohol in their bodies, the Howataka people take on new life, their bodies become healthy and strong, their minds clear and sharp. In the evening, Yuji has the Chief assemble all the Villagers around a communal bonfire. The Howataka people bask in the light of the fire and the warmth of the flames, as Howataka Elders and veteran warriors tell stories of old that inspire courage, honour, and wisdom. The speakers share the Tribe's stories handed down from generation to generation. The men, women, youth, and children, listen intently to inspiring stories that help to reshape and restore good views about themselves. After three months, Yuji, Otter, and the Ninjans prepare to leave to return to their Shoshone Camp. As they sit upon their horses, The Howataka Chief, Elders, Warriors, and people, bid them farewell expressing their gratitude. Yuji and the Ninjans bow respect to their temporary hosts. The people watch the Ninjans as they ride out of Camp and onto the Plains, going over hills to disappear from sight. One veteran warrior turns to the Chief and asks, "We are stronger and better! We are the Howataka as we once were. It is good!" The Elders and braves nearby, nod their heads, their eyes full of pride that Howataka Tribal honour has been restored. The brave looks out at the horizon to where the

Ninjans last were, and enquires, "Those warriors had good hearts and good spirits! (Pause) How will we know them in our songs and stories?" The Chief is quiet for a few seconds, then replies in a confident tone, "We will call them the **Black Riders!**"

# CHAPTER TWENTY-EIGHT
## *A New Dawn*

Other Tribes across the Plains hear of the Howatakas, and marvel how the devastated Tribe recovered to regain their place of strength and honour. Accounts are shared of the way the Black Riders helped the Village people - instilling courage to stop drinking, nursing sick ones back to health, hunting and fishing to provide food for families, and being examples of goodness, care, and respect. What began as a couple isolated requests, has become a common cry from Indian Tribes across the Plains - "Send us Ninjans!" The reason for this is connected to the many young braves, who once rode in the War Party, and now have returned to their Tribal home. Many of the Chiefs, Elders, and veteran warriors, do not know how to handle the wild braves, who are restless, rambunctious, and sometimes rebellious. Having learned how the Ninjans helped the Howatakas, the other Tribes want the same kind of assistance in their Villages.

At a Council Fire with the central tepee packed with Shoshone warriors, Buffalo Sky and the Elders discuss ways to help the other Tribes. Yuji, Otter and the Ninjans sit in a section near the leadership circle. Chief Buffalo Sky asks Yuji, "How many Ninjans do we have?" Yuji replies, "My Chief, our Ninjans number 37 warriors." The old warrior exchanges eye contact with the Elders, then comments, "We do not have enough Ninjans for every Tribe. (Pause) If we send 4 Ninjans to 8 different Tribes needing the most help - that will be a start!" Everyone thinks on the Chief's words. Buffalo Sky looks at Yuji and Otter and questions, "Will 4 Ninjans be able to help a Tribal Village?" Yuji and Otter exchange eye-contact, and Otter responds, "2 Ninjans are enough - 4 Ninjans will give strong help!" The young Ninjan

Master's words cause the Chief and Elders to ponder and discuss the approach. After a lengthy time of Council, Chief Buffalo Sky lifts his arm in the air and loudly proclaims, "We will send 4 Ninjans to each Tribe that need help. Our Ninjan warriors will stay 3 moons, then return to us." The Elders and warriors nod in agreement. The Shoshone braves begin to beat drums and chant. The assembly of warriors lift their voices to sing and celebrate the new venture to assist the other Indian Tribes!

Riders are dispatched with news from Buffalo Sky to the other Chiefs. Yuji, Otter, and the Ninjans, prepare for departure from their families and Shoshone Village. Each Ninjan is dressed in their black outfit, fitted with weapons, tools, and potions. The braves bid farewell to their loved ones, and gather to leave from the central tepee. Prior to this, Yuji and Otter, divided the Ninjans into separate groups based on each Ninjans knowledge, skills, and ability. The 8 Ninjan teams are waiting on horseback, ready to ride to their designated Indian Tribe, chosen by Buffalo Sky, the Elders, Yuji, and Otter. The Ninjan warriors understand the important role they will play. Each one will represent the Shoshone Tribe, and the Ninjan Oath they took before Yuji and Otter. The horses paw the ground, the mounts smell the open Plains, they are primed and ready to race over the grasslands. The entire Shoshone Village has gathered to see the departure of their Ninjan warriors. Chief Buffalo Sky emerges from the large tepee. He looks at the Ninjan groups, raises his arms, and declares loudly, "Our Ninjan brothers - show Goodness, Strength, and Honour. Help the Tribe. Respect them." The Shoshone Villagers release SHOUTS and VICTORY CRIES! Yuji and Otter observe their Ninjans ride out in separate teams - each group heads to a different Tribe spread across the Great Plains.

Days and weeks go by, and time moves from the First Moon - to the Second Moon - and toward the Third Moon. Periodic word comes back to the Shoshone Camp regarding the positive contributions made by the Ninjans. Wayward young braves are mentored to be noble warriors, herbal teas and Ninjan potions stop the craving for alcohol, Parents receive supportive guidance, and rambunctious teens and young people harness their energy into chores, training, and games. The Ninjans instruct Tribal warriors in basic Ninjan fighting skills and techniques for defence, and if necessary - offence. When the Third Moon arrives and passes, the Ninjan group in each of the Tribe prepares to depart for home. As the special warriors leave the various Villages and Camps, that Tribe's people shower the Ninjans with appreciation and pleasant farewells. Many of the Ninjan receive personal Tribal gifts as an expression of gratitude. Returning back at the Shoshone Camp, the Ninjans are officially welcomed by Chief Buffalo Sky, the Elders, Yuji, Otter, and the entire Shoshone Village. The Ninjans that left months ago, return as Heroes in the eyes of their Tribe's leaders and people. The entire Camp, young and old, men and women, fill the air with…

**HAPPY OUTBURSTS!  JUBILANT SHOUTS!  VICTORY CRIES!**

In the following years to come, Tribal Chiefs and Elders from across the Plains, send their select braves to be taught by Ninjans in the Shoshone Camp. Yuji, the respected Ninjan Master, strongly believes that braves from other Tribes should be trained to become Ninjans. Yuji understands that when other Tribe's have their own Ninjan warriors - the Indian Tribes of the Great Plains will greatly benefit, their Ninjans will help to uphold their Tribe's Pride and Honour. As Time passes, Ninjans do become established in the different Tribes, and trainees arise to become Ninjan Masters among their own people. Indian Nations of the Wild West embracing the Skills, Knowledge, and Wisdom, of the Far East!

All this begins the **Dawn of a New Day**!

THE END

www.ingramcontent.com/pod-product-compliance
Lightning Source LLC
Chambersburg PA
CBHW051233210726
48290CB00003B/936